FLASH FRY, PRIVATE EYE

Other Avon Camelot Books by
Tim Schoch

CREEPS

TIM SCHOCH grew up in New Jersey and received a Bachelor of Arts degree in Drama from the University of Tampa in Florida. He has been a newspaperman, a full-time actor, and is currently Copy Chief for a major New York City publisher. His first novel for young readers, *Creeps*—an Avon Camelot book—continues to be a success in the U.S. and abroad. He has also written three adult mystery novels, dozens of articles and humorous pieces for newspapers and magazines, and more than 250 songs, which he has performed in a musical comedy act with his partner, Jerry Winsett. He lives with his wife, Wendy McCurdy, in New Jersey.

FLASH FRY, PRIVATE EYE

TIM SCHOCH

Pictures by Wally Neibart

AN AVON  CAMELOT BOOK

FLASH FRY, PRIVATE EYE is an original publication of Avon Books. This work has never before appeared in book form.

AVON BOOKS
A division of
The Hearst Corporation
1790 Broadway
New York, New York 10019

Library of Congress Cataloging in Publication Data

Schoch, Tim.
    Flash Fry, private eye.

    (An Avon Camelot book)
    Summary: Canine detective Scratch helps his young master Flash Fry investigate a feud between two amateur tricksters, who end up locked in a nasty duel in a supposedly haunted house.
    [1. Dogs—Fiction. 2. Magic tricks—Fiction. 3. Mystery and detective stories] I. Title.
PZ7.S36476F1 1986   [Fic]   86-7954

First Camelot Printing: October 1986

CAMELOT TRADEMARK REG. U.S. PAT. OFF. AND IN OTHER COUNTRIES, MARCA REGISTRADA, HECHO EN U.S.A.

Printed in the U.S.A.

OPM 10 9 8 7 6 5 4 3 2 1

For Wendy

One: Marybeth Brings a Mystery

Flash Fry, Private Eye, yawned. He was sitting at his office desk in the basement of his house. There was a handsome bulldog curled up on the floor beside him. That's me. My name's Scratch, Private Nose. I'm the brains of the outfit, only Flash doesn't know it.

We'd just come from the candy store, and I was resting my dogs. Flash was eating a huge chocolate bar. I was chewing a wad of banana bubble gum that I'd found on the sidewalk and washed with my tongue. I only blow bubbles when his back is turned. To him, see, I'm just a loyal doggie, the short, hairy buddy who follows him around. What he doesn't know won't hurt him.

It was summer. Saturday. Morning. The whole day was ahead of us, and we didn't have a case. Flash was tapping his foot out of boredom. I was clicking my nails like a typewriter.

"What now, Scratch?" Flash asked.

If I could talk human, I would have said something. But I can't, so I just kind of woofed.

I dropped the gum on the floor beside my bowl and stuck out my tongue to cool off.

I looked up at my boy. He'd just turned eleven-and-a-half and thought he was pretty cool. Now he was acting cool with his fat sneakers propped up on the wobbly card table he calls a desk. He was wearing that silly, wide-brimmed, green gangster hat that always rides on the back of his redheaded head. He made the huge hat fit by stuffing an entire *TV Guide* inside the band.

An oldtime, bright red Coke machine sat humming against the wall to his left. He reached out and cranked down the metal handle. An ice-cold bottle of grape soda thudded down. He drinks nothing but grape. He grabbed it, popped off the cap in the slot, and took a long, cool guzzle.

1

Me, I get a bowl of warm, dusty water in the corner.

"Where's the detective business?" Flash asked his soda bottle. "There has to be somebody in this town who needs help."

Flash picked up the morning newspaper and started flipping through. "Oh, boy, here's some trouble," he said. He read some more. "Oh, yeah. Spooky. I'll tell you, Scratch, you'll never catch me out by that old Doomer house. Know what happened there last night?"

I didn't woof or anything. I just rolled my eyes in his direction.

"Johnny and George Jones, those kids down the street, they actually went *inside* the freaky house. Ten minutes later, they came running and screaming out of the place, saying they saw a zombie!" Flash gulped. "Nope, you'll never catch me inside there."

For years, people and dogs around town have been saying strange things happen up in the empty old Doomer house. Eerie woooooooing moans. Loud, sudden crashes. Ghostly music late at night. And worse. Some say that a long time ago, a whole family was scared to death in there, including their dog. Naturally, I don't believe that—but you'll never catch me inside that house, either.

I wandered over to the stack of storm windows that were leaning against the wall. I smiled at myself in the glass. I liked what I saw. I'm solid white, except for the left side of my face, which is brown. Good-looking but mysterious. I flexed my right shoulder muscle and sucked my teeth. What a dog. A dog of dogs.

I laid my chin on my paws to think. The cool cement floor felt wonderful on my bare belly. I spread out and began to doze.

Three booming knocks filled the basement and woke me up. I couldn't help myself—I barked. I barked again.

"Quiet, Scratch. Could be a client. Look professional."

I took a seat at the bottom of the cellar steps. I tried to look casual but tough. At the top of the eight steps are two huge wooden doors that open onto the backyard. They were closed. I perked up my ears. I heard someone breathing on the other side of those doors. My stubby tail began to wag.

Flash quickly looked official behind his desk. "Come in," he said.

With a few creaks and a croak, one of the two doors opened.

2

A wide square of golden sunlight stretched down into the room. A girl came down the steps, squinting into the dark basement. As she walked past me, I took a sniff of the bottom of her jeans and her sock. I knew immediately that she had a tabby cat, that she'd walked through the woods to get here, that both her jeans and socks were washed with Rainbow laundry detergent, that she'd had pancakes for breakfast, and that she was sweating lightly and was probably very nervous. If I'd used both nostrils, I could have found out more.

Flash was on his feet. He stuck out his hand, motioning to the onion crate in front of his desk. "Please," he said, grinning like a jerk, "have a seat, miss."

The girl nodded and looked behind her before she sat. She was about ten years old. She had frizzy blond hair and was blue-eyed and blushing. She wore a yellow T-shirt, and her hands were balling up the bottom of it. Something was squirming around in her mind.

"I'm Flash Fry," Flash said, leaning back in his chair. "Who's paying me a visit?"

The girl's eyes darted around the basement.

"Don't worry," Flash said, "we're alone."

What am I, the Invisible Dog?

I trotted along the floor and put my chin on the girl's lap. She liked that. She stroked my head. I liked that. I licked a spot of maple pancake syrup off the palm of her hand. She wasn't thrilled with that.

"Well," she said, "I know you, but we've never really met, because I go to the elementary school. I'm Marybeth Hurthwurst, Pete's sister."

"Oh, yeah, sure," Flash said, nodding like crazy.

He'd never heard of her.

"Yeah." Flash giggled. "Your brother is the best practical joker in the world. He put chattering teeth in the principal's desk drawer! What a riot. It must be fun to have a brother like that."

Marybeth's face was burning red. "Loads of fun, just loads," she said. I knew she didn't mean it.

"Ugly bulldog," Marybeth said, looking at me. "But cute."

An accurate description, but not quite the way I would have put it.

"Thanks. His name is Scratch. Would you like a soda?"

"No, thank you," she said.

3

As for me, I'd give my ears for a soda. Fat chance, though.

"So, what's your problem, Miss Hurthwurst?" Flash asked.

"It's Pete," she said. "I'm very worried about him."

Terrific, I thought. We need a good crime case, but what do we get instead? A worrier. I left her lap, sprawled on the floor, and gave her my bored look.

"Tell me about it," Flash said.

"Well," she began, "Pete's missing."

"Missing?" Flash said. "How long has he been missing?"

"I don't know," Marybeth said.

"Then how do you know he's missing at all?"

"Because he's not home."

"How long has he not been home?" Flash asked.

She shrugged. "I don't know."

Flash grunted. He was getting flustered. "Maybe he's not really missing. Maybe he's just out for a walk or something."

Marybeth shook her head back and forth.

"Why not?" Flash asked.

"His bed wasn't slept in last night," she said.

"Anything else? Any other clues?"

"Yes," she said. "My parents don't know where he is."

Flash huffed and took off his hat. "Anything *else?*"

"Yes. On his dresser is a pad. On the pad he'd written two words." She fell silent.

"Well?" Flash said. "What were the words?"

Marybeth swallowed. "The first word was *pond.*"

"Pond," Flash said. He rubbed his chin as if he had whiskers. "Hmmm. Pond. I wonder what that means. Hmmm." He thought it over.

I'd been keeping my eye on this Marybeth Hurthwurst. There was something about her I didn't trust. First of all, she was a cat lover. I never trust a cat lover. There was more, but I didn't know what it was. I'd have to wait and see. I scratched behind my ear, snorted, and rolled it over in my brain.

Finally, Flash spoke. "What was the second word?"

Marybeth's face suddenly scrinched up. At first I thought maybe Flash had kicked her under the desk or something, but that wasn't it. She was scared. Plenty scared.

"Well? What was the second word?" Flash asked when she calmed down.

Her face grew red, and she said, *"Brick."*

"Brick. Hmmm. Brick," Flash said. Then *his* face grew red.

4

"Oh, no. Not Brick. Not *Brick Glick!*" Flash almost fell over backward.

I hopped to my feet, ready to go. I barked twice, but nobody paid any attention to me.

Brick Glick! Brick Glick is a troublemaker, a double-trouble troublemaker. He picks on kids. He picks on dogs. He probably even picks on bunny rabbits. What could be worse than a bully like that? I'll tell you what's worse. He's a magician, too.

"What if—what if—what if—" Marybeth was trying to say something. "What if Brick Glick did something to Pete at the pond? Or—or turned him into a squirrel!"

"Nuts!" Flash said. "I'll take the case!"

It's about time.

"Oh, good!" Marybeth said. "I don't know how much I can pay you. All I have is a quarter right now."

Flash smiled and blinked. "You've already got enough to worry about, Marybeth. We'll talk money later. Besides, Pete is kind of a friend of mine, even though he once put a rubber frog in my milk. Listen, I'll go down to the pond and see what I can find. You meet us back here at noon sharp, got it?"

"Noon? Okay. Noon. I'll be here. Thanks, Flash."

"Forget it. We haven't got a second to lose. Scratch, let's go."

I was already going.

Once outside in the bright, hot sunshine, we said good-bye to Marybeth Hurthwurst. I lifted my leg against the hedge, then kicked some grass over it to cover my scent—in this business, you can't be too careful.

Flash got his huge green hat all twisted up in the laundry hanging on the clothesline—Flash's clothes dryer broke yesterday, and his dad had pinned up the clothes just before dark last night so they could get nice and soggy and buggy overnight. Finally, Flash wrestled free, and we headed toward the woods.

The grass was wet, and I snorted water up my nose as I tried to sniff out Pete's trail. We soon entered the shade of the thick woods.

Flash tripped on a fallen branch and fell onto a mound of moss. I licked his face and nudged him to his feet. He'd never survive without me.

Two: Tots in a Tree

I love the woods. The cool, dark, bird-chirping shade felt terrific on my pads. I pranced around, sniffed a black beetle, chased my tail a little to get Flash laughing, then smashed my way through some bushes. Flash swatted at something near his face and smacked his cheek instead. I laughed, but he didn't know it.

We were supposed to be going to the pond, so that's where I was trying to lead Flash. But he kept wanting to zag over to the right. The heck with him, I thought. I just kept on going straight until he got tired of calling me and followed in my direction. Humans are weird.

I love the woods, did I tell you that? I love to sniff everything—all the great smells go right up my nose into my eyes! I knew Flash couldn't smell too much of anything, and I felt sorry for him. I took a long time sniffing a really wonderful mound of blue-green moss. I also got excited being around all those trees. I think you understand why.

After my fifth tree, Flash screamed in a whisper. "Who's that?" He was looking up ahead. He dove behind a fallen log.

Big deal. I knew there were people up there fifteen minutes ago. If Flash were a dog, he would have smelled their footprints a half-mile away. Smelly sneakers. Two kids: one boy, one girl. They were up in a treehouse, and I could hear their giggling. Flash couldn't hear a thing.

So I made myself comfortable between a couple of tree roots and waited until Flash decided to find out who was up there.

Sometimes I really wish I could talk to him. Sure would save a lot of time. I can think in human talk, but every time I open my yap to try to talk, only barks come out. Can't figure it out. I used to get really frustrated, but now I'm used to it.

6

Gotta accept yourself for what you are. It could be worse: I could have been born a slug. Arroo!

Flash didn't feel like moving just yet. Me, I was getting tired of sitting around and panting. Besides, we had a mystery to solve, a missing kid to find. I looked toward Flash and gave him a hurry-up bark.

"*Shhhh!*" he said. "Scratch, shut up. Come here."

I looked at him like I didn't understand what in heck he just said.

"Here, boy. Come here, boy. Come on, Scratch." He made snicking sounds with his tongue and little squeaky sounds with his lips. Believe me, if you want a dog to come to you, don't do that.

I could see no good reason to go with him. What if I did? Then we'd both hide? I stood up, stretched, then trotted toward the treehouse.

"Scratch, stop!" Flash whispered. "It might be Brick Glick!"

Ah-ha! So that's what he was afraid of. I knew it wasn't Brick up in that treehouse, but how could I tell Flash? I couldn't. He'd just have to suffer until he got brave enough to follow me.

I sat at the bottom of the tall tree and looked up toward the treehouse. The treehouse was a great one, with a roof and everything. In fact, it reminded me of home—my doghouse. If I could climb trees, this would be perfect for me. Oh, well.

I smiled at the two faces looking down at me. At least, I thought I was smiling. Whenever I open my mouth and pant, people always say I'm smiling. What I'm really doing is waiting to burp.

"Hi, doggie," the girl said. Her long blond hair was swaying over her face in the breeze. It was making me dizzy.

"Hey, mutt! Come on up! Jump!" said the boy, laughing like crazy.

Very funny. I didn't like the boy right off. I stopped smiling. I barked at him, and he laughed some more.

"Darn it, Scratch, why don't you come when I call?" Flash, my fearless master, finally decided to join me.

I shook my head and walked around the tree, sniffing for evidence. I didn't find anything except a thousand-legger. I left it alone.

"Hey, kids," Flash called up. "What are you doing up there?"

7

What did he think they were doing up there? Bowling?

"Playing!" the boy yelled down.

"Oh," Flash said. "Have you seen two guys around here lately?"

The kids disappeared inside. I could hear them whispering and giggling. If Flash hadn't been shuffling around in the leaves, I might have heard what they were saying.

"Yeah," the boy said. "We see everything. We're spies. We spy all day. We saw two guys. We see squirrels, too, and you're nuts!"

Flash was so excited he ignored the insult. "You really saw two guys? You really did?"

The boy ducked back inside to talk to the girl, then he stuck out his head and said, "No!"

"Hey, you just said you saw them. Did you, or didn't you?" Flash asked them. "One of the guys was probably dressed in black. His name is Brick Glick. Know him? Seen him?"

"No!" the kids said together.

"The other guy is Pete Hurthwurst."

"No!" the kids yelled again. Then they giggled again.

Flash scratched his head. "Have you been up there all morning?"

"No!"

"Were you here last night?"

"No!"

"So you just got here?"

"No!"

"Well, when did you get here?"

"No!"

I wished there was some way to get those kids to talk. Anyone who goes to the pond would probably go right by them. They must have seen Pete or Brick or anyone else who had gone down there. But the kids weren't talking. Oh, well.

"No!"

The kids were having a ball, but Flash wasn't giving up. I sneezed, licked my nose, shook my head, and began wandering deeper into the woods toward the pond. I chased and snapped at a yellow butterfly, then looked back. Flash was finally coming. He paused, turned, shook his fist at the kids, then followed me.

Score: KIDS 1, FLASH 0.

9

"Those kids are lying," Flash said. "They know something. I just know they do."

I knew it, too.

So we headed toward the pond. And what we soon found there would start Flash Fry's biggest adventure ever.

Three: A Clue by a Canoe

A nice light breeze was ruffling my fur, and I hung my tongue out so the breeze could cool my throat. I saw a rabbit and stared at it until it saw me and hopped away like a frog.

Soon we came to a narrow, worn-down path.

"This must lead to the pond!" Flash said. "Maybe Pete came here to go fishing or something and just fell asleep. Maybe he caught a whale and was dragged out to the ocean. Maybe..."

Brilliant, isn't he?

My nose already smelled out that this path led right to the pond. I also heard a fish jump and a snake hiss.

Flash ran ahead of me down the path like he was in charge. I let him.

Soon we were standing near the edge of the pond beside a rotting, sunken canoe. I could barely see over the top of the reeds to the still, brown water. The pond was surrounded by tall trees and was alive with noise that only I could hear. A turtle slipped into the water about twenty feet away. A snake out in the middle made a grab for a gnat. Somewhere on the other shore, water was gurgling into the pond from a stream. And a hundred million little tiny bugs were all humming different tunes. The whole place smelled like musky, wet freshness.

All was very quiet until Flash yelled, "Hey!" Birds flew scared-out-of-their-minds from the trees. I almost slipped into the water. Hair was standing up behind my head.

"Scratch, look what I found!"

I looked. It was a small, old black book called *Magic of the Masters*. Flash found it by a bush near the canoe. I tried to get a close sniff of the book, but Flash held it away.

Flash opened the book and flipped through a few pages. He whistled. "Magic tricks! And they're so complicated that I

11

can't even understand them. And look who wrote his name in the front. Brick Glick. Brick's magic book! Brick was here! Brick's our man! This is proof!"

Flash looked all around, then just stopped still and pushed his wide-brimmed green hat to the back of his head. "Hold it," he said. "But how do we know that Pete was here, too? Hmmmmm." He began searching again.

While Flash was twisting his mind inside out, I wandered down and took a few laps from the pond. Not bad. Then I sniffed for tracks. There were so many odors around there that all I smelled were flowers, mud, animal droppings, and rotting reeds. I thought I got a whiff of a sneaker, but I wasn't sure.

Flash looked stumped, and I felt sorry for him. I rubbed up against his leg, and he stroked my head. Ahhh.

Then I saw something. I left Flash, scampered toward the canoe where the book had been, picked something up in my lips, walked back to Flash, and spat it in his hand.

"Yuk!" Flash said. "Why'd you give me this disgusting, gigantic, dead horsefly? Yuk!"

He tossed it away.

I picked it up and gave it back to him.

"Stop it, Scratch! You—" Flash took a good look at the horsefly. "Hey. This is rubber. Hey! It's a fake fly! *Hey!* It must be one of Pete's jokes—so he *was* here! And he was here with Brick Glick, because here's Brick's book! Hold it. Let me think about this."

I snuck in under his arm, and he petted my ear and tugged it a little. Ahhh. I crawled over his legs and kind of rolled onto my side so he could rub my tummy.

"Maybe," Flash said, "Brick wasn't here. Maybe Pete left both the giant horsefly and the book. But what would Pete be doing with Brick's book? No, Brick had to be here, didn't he? Hmmmm. Marybeth will be coming to our house at noon. We still have time. There's only one thing to do. Come on, Scratch, let's go have a talk with Brick Glick. Maybe we can wrap this case up."

Flash got up just as I was dropping into a dream about trees and fields and running and bones.

Flash stuck the magic book in his back pocket, then bolted up the path with one hand holding down his immense hat. Me, I yawned. I took a few more quick sniffaroonies, then followed.

When we got to the treehouse again, the kids were already

giggling. Before Flash could say anything to them, they both stuck their little bratty faces out and shouted, "No!"

After Flash had raced ahead, the little boy whispered down to me, "Hey, mutt. We did see somebody by the pond, we really did. And if you weren't a dumb dog, you could go tell Flash. But you can't! Ha-ha!"

I *knew* they'd seen something. I'm not dumb, but the brats were right—I couldn't tell Flash. What could I do? I lifted my leg against their tree, then left.

Four: Brick Glick's Tricks

We went home, got Flash's old three-speed bike, then took off. Lots of fun for me when Flash rides his bike, know what I mean? I've got to run my tail off to keep up with him. Marathon mutt, that's me. What I need are sneakers.

I hated the thought of facing Brick Glick. Too many times that jerk had thrown rocks and sticks at me for no good reason except that he's so mean. I've never bitten anyone, but I'm telling you, I came real close to taking a chunk out of Brick Glick a couple of times. But I didn't. I have good taste. And I knew he'd taste awful.

I also knew that if it came down to it, I might have to protect Flash from Brick Glick. I started practicing looking vicious. I tried to foam at the mouth, but all I did was drool on my paws.

When Brick Glick's house was in sight, Flash got off his bike. He was shaking. He was scared. He was shaking so hard that I could hear his knees slapping against the inside of his jeans. But I've got to hand it to Flash, once he's on a case, he doesn't stop.

"Aw," he said, "let's forget it."

I bumped him a couple of times with my nose, and we began walking up the path to Brick Glick's front door. His house was maroon with white trim. The freshly mowed lawn smelled great. I wanted to roll on it, but now wasn't the time. Flash needed me.

Flash dropped his bike on the lawn and walked up to the front door. He knocked five times. Actually, he only knocked four times, because on his fifth knock, the door opened and he knocked on air.

There stood Brick Glick. He was wearing black jeans and a black long-sleeved baseball shirt with a red number 13 on the front and back. But his baseball shirt was too big for him, and his jeans were three inches too long. I guess Brick thought he was bigger than he really is. He didn't look so scary to me. In fact, he looked kind of silly.

Brick Glick put his hands on his hips. His shirt came out of his pants, and I could see his BVDs. He laughed. "Well, it's Flash Fry and his silly hat and dumb dog. What do you want?"

"I—I—I," Flash said.

Atta boy, I thought, show Brick you're not scared.

"I was practicing my magic," Brick Glick said. "So make it fast. Want me to turn your ugly bulldog into a bullfrog?"

He raised a long finger in my direction. I showed him my teeth, but I don't think they frightened him.

"No!" Flash said.

"Then tell me what you want," Brick Glick said.

"Where's Pete?" Flash said.

"Who?"

"Pete Hurthwurst. He's missing, and I think you know where he is. Where is he?"

Brick Glick chuckled. "You and your stupid detective cases crack me up, Fry. Think I will turn your pooch into a bullfrog."

"You wouldn't dare," Flash said. "Besides, you can't do it, anyway."

"A challenge? Oh, boy. I love challenges. Watch this!" With a quick flick of his skinny wrist, a whole bunch of flowers suddenly appeared in his hand. "Nature, right out of thin air!"

"They're paper," Flash said. "The flowers are paper."

Brick Glick blushed. His trick was ruined. "Paper? Ha!"

"Let me see them."

"Too late!" Brick Glick said, and with another flick, the flowers were gone.

Take it from me, folks, they were paper flowers. No smell. Silly Brick Glick was beginning to bore me. So what? I thought. Turn me into a bullfrog; I'm getting some shut-eye. I curled up at Flash's feet and began to doze, keeping one eye on the dumbo magician. Dogs can do that.

"Have you lost anything recently?" Flash asked.

"I'm about to lose my temper with you, smallfry Fry."

"A book, for instance?"

"My magic book? You found it? Come on, give it back."

"Sorry, it's evidence now, Brick. This is no stupid case. Pete is missing. I think he disappeared by the pond. And that's where I found your book. So that probably means you were there, too. I'll ask again, where's Pete?"

"And I'll tell you again, if you don't stop this stuff, you'll be at the pet store tonight buying frog food. I want my magic book, Fry. Now." Brick held out his hand. His too-long sleeve slid down and drooped over his fingers.

Flash shook his head. "I'll give it back when the case is closed. And stop saying you'll turn Scratch into a frog. You know you can't."

Brick Glick bent over, then rose very quickly. "A ball!" In his hand was a small red rubber ball. He quickly tossed it above Flash's head, and it exploded in a whirl of green smoke and red glitter. Unfortunately, there was a breeze blowing, and most of the glitter fell all over Brick Glick's curly hair and on his lips.

Flash laughed. "Nice trick, Brick."

Brick was spitting glitter off his lips. Then he swung his hand up to Flash's face. Flash ducked. "Silver dollars!" One silver dollar appeared between Brick's fingers. He twitched his hand and another was there. Then another. Then four.

Flash snatched the silver dollars out of Brick Glick's hand.

"Hey! Give them back!"

"Nope," Flash said. He'd gotten his courage back. "I'll give them back when you tell me where Pete Hurthwurst is."

"How should I know where he is? I haven't seen Pete in days, and I never go down to that stinking pond."

"Then what was your magic book doing down there?"

"Beats me," Brick said with a shrug. "It was stolen last week. It is my most prized possession. Don't read it! It's very dangerous for anyone other than a true magician to read the secret magic of the masters. I want it back, Fry, and I'll get it back at all costs. Remember that."

"Sorry, I need it for evidence. Who do you think stole it?"

"Don't really know. But it kind of looks like that creep Pete stole it, doesn't it? Kind of looks like he's trying to get me in trouble, too."

Flash scratched his head. "Maybe he is. Wonder why. Wonder where he is now."

Brick Glick smiled. "Some detective you are. Now give me back my silver dollars."

Flash handed Brick Glick the silver dollars. Brick grabbed

them, then tossed them at the ground. They each hit with a flap and bounced off into his yard.

"What'd you do that for?" Flash asked.

Brick blushed. "They were supposed to explode. Wonder what went wrong."

Flash giggled. "Some magician you are."

Brick frowned. "Don't make fun of me, Fry, or I'll give you some real magic with this." He held up his fist.

Flash gulped.

"You have my book, and I'm mad, Fry. And if you see Pete, tell him he's in big trouble for stealing my book and trying to get me in trouble. But, right now, I have to get back to practicing my magic." He picked up his silver dollars from the lawn, then paused in the doorway. "This silver dollar trick didn't work. But some of them do. Like this!"

Suddenly, there was a flash of light and a huge puff of thick, black smoke. And Brick Glick was gone. Flash now stood before an empty doorway with his mouth hanging open and his eyes popping out. Then the front door closed all by itself.

Flash and I were home in about three seconds.

Five: Jokes, Ice, and Lies

Flash put Brick Glick's magic book downstairs, behind his desk, on a shelf marked EVIDENCE.

"Boy, is Brick weird," Flash said to himself as he paced and thought.

Me, I could have used a dog biscuit about now. Better yet, a candy bar.

"Hold it," Flash said. "There's a clue staring me right in the face, and I couldn't even see it."

I knew what he was going to say: We have to see Pete Hurthwurst.

"What if Brick is lying? What if he did see Pete at the pond? There's only one way to find out. We have to see if Pete Hurthwurst is home."

I knew it.

"Come on, Scratch!"

Flash grabbed his bike. This time he put me in the newspaper basket on the front handlebars. I love it when he gives me a ride. I love to lick the wind whipping in my face. We took off.

To get to Pete's house, we had to follow the path that skirted through the woods and led a little ways up the hill to where the big houses are. Mansions. Pete's dad is loaded.

As we were rolling by the woods, we saw a familiar sight. A treehouse.

"Gotta try one more time," Flash mumbled to himself. "If I could get an eyewitness who saw Brick with Pete, I'd have this case wrapped up tight." He stopped the bike, dumped me out, and headed toward the tree. I followed with a sigh.

The kids were still in the treehouse. They were eating potato chips—I could hear and smell them. When they saw us, they started giggling.

"Hey, kids," Flash yelled up. "Ready to tell me who you saw by the pond?"

"Yes!" the little boy yelled down.

"Great. Who'd you see? Was it Brick Glick?"

"Yes!"

"Terrific. Was Pete Hurthwurst with him?"

"Yes!"

"Oh, boy. Was anyone else with them?"

"Yes!"

"Who? Tell me who was with them!"

"Santa Claus!" And the kids giggled like monkeys in a tree.

Strange kids. If we could only stop them from playing their dumb games, we could get the truth out of them.

Flash shook his fist at them, loaded me back into his bike basket, and took off toward Pete's house.

We soon zoomed into Pete's huge driveway. His house looked like a modern castle. Four floors. Wide, wide, wide. All white. We ran up to the front door. Flash had a hard time finding the doorbell, but soon he did. It was a knob you pull out. He pulled it. Immediately, the large, heavy door creaked open.

"Hey, what do you know! It's Flash!"

The person who answered the door was Pete Hurthwurst, practical joker, Flash's on-again-off-again buddy, and not one of my favorite people in the world, because he plays practical jokes on dogs, too.

Pete's not a bad-looking kid: trimmed dirty-blond hair, dark eyes, nice smile, clean clothes, rich-kid clothes.

"You're here!" Flash said.

"You've got good eyes, Flash," Pete said. "Come on in. I'll get you something to drink. Bring your dog. It's okay."

Gee, thanks.

We walked inside his huge house. The ceiling was so high that I had to sit to see it. In front of us was a wide staircase with deep red carpeting. Rich-looking, deep green furniture was in the room to my left. The house was so clean that all I could smell was the scent of some kind of polish. No place for a dog who likes to roll in grass and prance in mud.

"I've got some questions for you," Flash said to Pete. "I can't believe you're really here."

Pete looked at Flash like he was nuts. "Come on," he said, "we'll go to my room."

We headed toward the red stairs. My nails clicked loudly on the marble floor. I sounded big.

Before we got to the stairs, a tall thin man appeared from I

20

don't know where. He wore a short, black coat, white shirt, bow tie, and black pants and shoes. He reeked of polish and garlic. The polish told me he was the butler, and the garlic told me he'd just come from the kitchen.

Before he spoke, he stopped in his tracks and looked down at me. For a minute, I thought he was going to polish me. Instead, he just rolled his eyes and sighed.

"Anything, sir?" he wheezed to Pete.

"Root beer for myself and Flash. Water for the dog."

"Yes, sir."

"Thank you, Rowland."

The butler left.

Need I point out that the boys get root beer and I get water? For revenge, I scratched out a big ball of fur and watched it tumble across the floor toward the kitchen.

We went upstairs to Pete's room, which looked almost as big as a gym. The room was blue and had everything a boy could ever want, including two video game machines in the corner.

Flash kept saying, "Wow! Wow! Wow!"

The guys headed for two blue chairs by the window. When Flash sat in his chair, it made a loud *BRRRRRRRRRP!* sound, and Flash leaped up. Pete was laughing like crazy as Flash took the Whoopie cushion from under the pillow on the chair seat.

"Funny," Flash said. "Very funny."

"I know!" Pete said.

Pete never stops playing his tricks.

I made myself comfortable on a big floor pillow and felt like snoozing immediately. But I had to stay awake. I had to hear what Pete had to say.

I smelled Rowland before he knocked. He knocked sharply two times, then marched in with a tray. He gave the boys their tall mugs of delicious root beer, then placed a big silver bowl on the floor for me. Inside the bowl was water. And ice cubes. Ice cubes! What a treat! I love chewing ice! I looked up at Rowland, and he winked at me. I tried to wink back, then started lapping.

"Will that be all, sir?"

"Thank you," Pete said.

Rowland left.

"Look. Your dog likes ice," Pete said, laughing at me crunching away. I was in ecstacy.

21

Everybody drank for a moment.

"Hey!" Flash yelled, brushing off his shirt.

Pete was laughing like a monkey. "Got ya!"

"A dribble glass!" Flash said, looking at his glass. "It's got a hole in it!"

"Here," Pete said, giggling. "Here's a real glass."

"Thanks a heap, creep."

"Hey," Pete said, "look at your dumb dog."

I was chasing an ice cube across the floor. Every time I tried to pick it up, it squirted out. I did this about ten times. Finally, I sucked it in and brought it back to the pillow. Then I realized I was drooling on the pillow. Then I felt guilty and tried to lick off the melted ice. That made it worse, and it got fuzzies on my tongue. I took a drink of water to wash down the fuzzies, and I drooled on the pillow again. This could go on forever. The heck with it. Crunch. Crunch. Ice. Mmmmmmmm.

"So," Pete said, "how've you been? What's up? What's down? What's what?"

"Is your sister home?"

"Marybeth? Nope. She bolted this morning. Don't know where she is. Why?"

"She came to see me today."

"Really? What for?"

"She told me you disappeared last night. She said you were missing."

"Lies. I'm right here. I've been here all night. What else did she say?"

"She said she found a note in your room that said *pond* and *Brick*."

"I don't believe it."

I stopped crunching. What was going on? Just what was going on?

"Don't believe a word Marybeth says," Pete said. "She's always doing dumb things to get me in trouble because I play practical jokes on her. She's always getting me punished. And now she's lying to you."

"So we went to the pond. We found Brick Glick's magic book. We also found one of your huge rubber horsefly gags. Then I talked to Brick, who said he didn't know anything. I figured maybe you . . . or you and Brick . . . or Brick and you . . . I don't know what to think!"

22

"Listen," Pete said. "Believe me, I was never at the pond. I was right here all night. And I never see Brick Glick. I even close my eyes when I pass him at school. If anybody sees Brick Glick, it's Marybeth."

"Huh?" Flash said. He pushed back his green gangster hat. "She said she doesn't know Brick."

"She lied. She met him around the neighborhood and went over to see his magic tricks one night. She came back bawling."

"Crying?"

"Yeah. Crying really hard. I felt sorry for her, too. Brick must have done something horrible to her. Even though my sister's a brat, she didn't deserve being picked on by Brick. Brick's an A-1 jerk."

I made a mental note: Pete hates Brick.

Flash sat back. He looked shocked. "Let me get this straight. You were never missing. There was no note. You were never at the pond, never lost a horsefly, and didn't steal Brick's book."

"Who said I stole Brick's book?"

"Brick did. But he was only guessing. What a strange case. Marybeth must have lied about everything."

"Doesn't surprise me," Pete said, finishing off his root beer. "But why'd she lie? What could my crazy sister be up to?"

"Wish I knew," Flash said. "Hope I didn't get Brick mad for nothing."

I hoped he didn't, either. Me, I was also wondering about who really stole Brick's magic book and why. Could it have been Pete? Or did Marybeth steal it when she went over to Brick's house? As Flash would say, hmmmm.

Then I saw something scoot past the door. I'd smelled it a few minutes before and had been watching out for it ever since. I snuck up to the door.

"Hey," Pete said. "Your dog's spotted Marybeth's cat. Hope he doesn't eat it."

Yuk! The cat took off. I let it go. I'd find it later. Cats see everything, and maybe this cat had a clue.

"So, Pete, do you have any ideas?"

"Nope. But I'll tell you, I'm gonna have a long talk with Marybeth."

"Yeah, me, too," Flash said. "I'll let you know if I find out anything. See ya, Pete."

23

"See ya. And if I hear anything, I'll let you know."

"Thanks."

"By the way," Pete said, "nice hat, Flash."

"You like it?"

"No."

They both laughed. We left.

We walked down the beautiful red stairs and out into the muggy air again. We started walking the bike back home. Flash was pretty upset. He hates to be confused.

"Marybeth said that she'd meet us at our house at noon. Come on, Scratch, we have twenty minutes. Just enough time to ask Brick Glick if Marybeth really went to his house that time."

Oh, no, not Brick's again. I didn't want to be turned into a bullfrog. I hate eating flies.

Just as we were rolling up to Brick Glick's house, a car backed out of his driveway. Brick Glick's mother was driving, and Brick Glick sat beside her, throwing sparkly stuff out the window. He saw us and shook his fist.

Whew.

We got home at noon on the dot. When we went downstairs to the basement, we discovered two things: A fat repairman in a green uniform was fixing the clothes dryer, and Marybeth wasn't there.

"She's just late, that's all," Flash said. "Let's wait. In fact, let's wait and eat."

Flash went upstairs, then came back down with some gooky food for me. I took some in my mouth. With one jerk of my head, I tossed it to the back of my tongue so I wouldn't have to taste it. Then I chewed it two times and swallowed it down.

Flash went to the small refrigerator in the corner, got out three circles of bologna, put two slices of American process cheese food on top of that, rolled them in a tube, and took a bite. He cranked the handle on the Coke machine and got his grape soda, then sat at his desk and munched.

The fat repairman glanced hungrily at Flash's food.

"Where is she?" Flash said ten minutes later.

Ten minutes after that, he said, "Where the heck *is* she?"

Fifteen minutes later, he said, "Know what, Scratch? I don't think she's coming."

The fat repairman looked down at me and said, "I think he's right." He packed up his tools and left.

24

"Maybe," Flash said, "Marybeth saw us go see Pete. Maybe she knows that we know she lied about Pete being missing. Maybe she's too embarrassed to come over. Sure wish I knew why she lied, though."

Me, too.

The phone rang.

"I'll get it!" Flash yelled upstairs to his Mom. He dove for the phone by the refrigerator. "Hello?"

"Hi, Flash," said the voice on the other end. "It's me. Marybeth."

I could hear her as if she were right next to me. I'm a dog, remember? Big ears. Handsome ears, too.

"Where are you?" Flash yelled. "I've been waiting here for you. I've got questions—"

"Sorry I'm late, Flash," Marybeth said. "In fact, I'm not coming at all. I have, um, a piano lesson and, um, more things to do. Plenty of things to do."

Lies, I thought. More lies.

"But—" Flash said.

"So I'll see you tomorrow, okay?" Marybeth said. "I'll see you first thing in the morning, I promise. I'll explain everything then."

"But—"

"Bye!"

Marybeth hung up.

Flash dropped the receiver in its cradle. He took his hand off the phone and wiped his brow.

"Great," he said. "Just great. I'll never solve the case this way. Great. Marybeth has lied about everything. I need answers, and now I have to wait until tomorrow. Great. Now what'll I do? Huh, Scratch? What will I do?"

Flash's Mom hollered from upstairs, "You can mow the lawn like you promised your father this morning."

Flash sighed. "Oh, great. Just great."

Six: Cat Talk

The next morning wasn't sunny, mainly because the sun hadn't come up—it was four A.M. I was all curled up and cozy on the warm covers at the foot of Flash's bed. Flash was shaking me, but I was pretending to be asleep.

"Come on, Scratch, get up!" Flash said, standing there in his underwear. "Marybeth said she'd be here first thing in the morning, and I want to be ready."

I opened one eye, but didn't move. Flash was hopping into his clothes like there was a fire or something.

"I've got a feeling I'm going to break this case wide open today," he said. "Even though Pete isn't really missing, I want to know why Marybeth lied and who stole Brick's magic book and left it by the pond with the rubber horsefly. Something strange is going on, and I have to know what it is. Let's go." And he rushed out of the bedroom.

The only reason I followed him was to make sure he wasn't sleepwalking. He wasn't.

Flash's basement office was damp and cool. Outside it was still dark. He flicked on his desk lamp and sat down to wait.

"Should be dawn soon," Flash said. "Marybeth ought to be here any minute."

I was so tired I couldn't even wag my tail. Even though I hated the thought of going outside, I had to go. I shuffled up to the basement door and just sat there. Flash quickly got the message and opened the door. I went outside, waited for my eyes to adjust to the dark, then headed for the nearest tree.

Suddenly, something burst out of the bushes, streaked across our backyard, then dove into the bushes on the other side.

The hair on the back of my neck stood straight up. I was so

scared I couldn't even bark. When I got my senses together, I realized what it was. It was Marybeth's cat, the one I'd seen when we visited Pete. What the heck was it doing running around at this hour of the morning? I decided to find out.

I quickly put my nose to the ground and followed the cat's scent through the bushes, around some garbage cans, through a garden, then under the neighbor's porch.

The wet tabby cat was huddled in a corner, shaking like it had seen a ghost. When it saw me, it raised one paw and popped its claws out. I didn't feel like having a crazy cat hanging all over my face, so I started backing up. The cat dropped its paw, tilted its head, then wiggled its nose.

I smiled and sat down.

Let me explain something to you humans out there. (You dogs already know this, so you can skip on down.) Okay. Dogs can talk to each other, but not in the way you think. Dogs can tell humans certain things by barking high or low, loud or soft, to show hunger, fear, whatever. But when dogs talk to dogs, they don't bark. Barks mean nothing dog to dog. If a dog barks at another dog, it is only out of excitement. Dogs talk in silence.

How do they do that, you ask? With their faces. Wiggling eyebrows—left, right, both, a little, a lot. It all means different things. Tongues—out all the way, halfway, inside the teeth, lolling off the right or left side, flapping. That all means different things, too. Noses—snorting, sniffing, wriggling, scrunching. All different.

I can't go into the whole language here. It is very complicated and involves tail wags, sitting and standing, ear lifts, head tilts, prancing, and plenty more. Neat, huh?

But for a dog, cats are harder to talk to. Cats have their own special language. But there are certain movements that all animals understand, and I was about to lay a few on this tabby cat of Marybeth's. Maybe it could tell me why it was racing around so early in the morning.

So I got comfortable. The disgusting cat had its back leg stuck up in the air and was licking itself. I couldn't look. Why do cats lick themselves instead of taking a nice hot bubble bath like a civilized dog?

Well, anyway, the cat stopped licking as soon as it saw I was sticking around. It backed itself against the wall, arched its back, and hissed. I hissed back. The cat laughed. Contact!

27

I wiggled my left ear. Snorted through my left nostril. And hung out my tongue.

The cat blinked its eyes, licked its whiskers, and rolled onto its back.

I had asked it why it was running around scared out of its tiny mind. I only caught one word of what it said back: *Lernoo*. What the heck does that mean?

After about fifteen minutes of trying to talk to the cat, my face was tired and the cat had fallen asleep. But I did learn one important thing: A few hours ago, in the middle of the night, Brick Glick had attacked Pete's house by throwing an enormous firework. The horrible explosion shattered Pete's bedroom window, and everybody in the house awoke screaming. The cat ran for its life.

I scratched my ear and thought. This was a dangerous development. You don't go around exploding other people's windows without something really bad happening. Why did Brick Glick do it? Had Pete or Marybeth done something to Brick first? Did Brick do it because his magic book was stolen and he was getting back at the thief? But who did he think he was getting back at—who *was* the thief?

The cat woke up and started licking itself again, so I left.

The sky was getting brighter. It would be daytime soon. Flash had said he might break the case today. Me, I thought that this might just turn out to be the worst day of Flash's life. I headed for home.

Flash was sound asleep, his face mashed onto the top of his desk. As soon as I flopped on the floor, I started snoring. Ahhh, wonderful sleep...

"Oh, no!"

Flash's yell woke me up from dreams of boneland. Outside it was a bright, sunny day.

"Look at the time!" Flash said, staring at his watch. "It's nine o'clock! Where's Marybeth?"

I yawned, giving Flash a good look at my teeth, tongue, and down my throat. My stomach growled.

Flash whirled around and started dialing the telephone.

"Hello?" Flash said. "Is Marybeth there? Yes, I know it's early. I'm sorry, but I have to talk with her. This is Flash Fry. Yes, I'll wait." Flash tapped his foot while he waited. "She's not home? Well, okay, thank you." Flash hung up. "Hmmm. Maybe she's on her way over here."

28

After waiting a half-hour without seeing Marybeth, Flash finally caught on that Marybeth wasn't coming. And he was mad.

"What's going on?" he said. "She never comes over when she says she will. Scratch, we've got to find her. Come on."

No way, I thought. I'm hungry. I'm not moving until I eat. I just sat there like a lump.

"Scratch, I said come on. Move it!"

Nope. My stomach was so empty that when it growled, it echoed. I looked at him like he was invisible.

Flash moved toward me. I knew he would have dragged me outside if his mother hadn't called him.

"Flash," she yelled from upstairs. "Come to breakfast. Pancakes. Come on, now. And don't forget to feed Scratch."

Goodie, goodie, goodie.

Flash sighed. "Well, even crime fighters have to eat, right, boy? Hey, where'd you go?"

I was already upstairs, prancing around my bowl with my stomach roaring and my tongue hanging almost on the floor.

Seven: This Means War!

Ahhh. Twenty-five minutes later, my stomach was full and very happy. I love breakfast, because I always get leftover toast and eggs and bacon. Flash's stomach was full, too, but he wasn't happy at all. It was almost ten o'clock in the morning, the sun was bright, and Flash didn't know what to do next.

"Now what?" he said. He kicked a stone from his driveway, and we both watched as it hopped and jumped down to the street and out into the road. A car roared by and ran over it.

I licked the last few tasty drops of breakfast off my chops and sat down to wait for him to make up his mind. I sure did wish I could tell Flash what the cat told me. Flash would probably decide to go look for Marybeth, but I thought we should go have another talk with Brick Glick.

"Okay," Flash said, clapping his hands. He adjusted his huge green hat and frowned. "We have to find Marybeth. Time for some legwork."

I'm good at legwork, much better than Flash. I've got two more legs. But, even if I had eight legs, I didn't think we'd find Marybeth by walking around.

"Let's go," Flash said.

He took three long strides, then stopped.

"If only I knew where to go," he said.

I sat. He thought. I was getting bored. Maybe there was time for a little more breakfast. My mouth began to water. No, better watch my weight.

A minute later, he said, "I've got it. Maybe if we took a walk at the scene of the so-called crime, I'd get some ideas."

Stinko idea, I thought. But the path toward the pond would take us near Brick Glick's house, and maybe I could get Flash to go over and question the weird kid about that explosion last night.

30

So we headed into the woods. I pranced ahead of him, used a few trees, then we heard a familiar voice.

"Hi, doggie!"

The kids in the treehouse were hanging out and laughing at us. They were wrapped in sleeping bags, and their hair was messy. What do they do, live up there?

"Aw, shut up, you brats," Flash yelled up.

"We know something you don't know," the little girl said.

"I doubt it," Flash said.

"Yes, we do," the boy said. "The whole neighborhood does."

That got to Flash. He stopped. "What do you mean?"

"It woke me up," the girl said.

"Me, too," the boy said.

"What did?" Flash asked.

The boy giggled. "Oh, it was terrible. Really loud, too."

"What? What? What?" Flash was so curious that he almost jumped up into the tree.

The boy shook his head. "Can't tell you."

"Tell me," Flash demanded.

"Nope," the girl said.

Flash stomped his foot on some moss. "Tell me!"

That got the kids laughing really hard.

"Go ask Brick Glick!" the boy finally said.

At last, the brats said something important. There they were, up in that treehouse, spying on the whole neighborhood. I had a feeling that they would be very important later on.

Flash turned and started walking straight for Brick Glick's house. He finally had something to do.

Flash and I walked right up to Brick Glick's front porch. Flash stood to the side and knocked. I sat beside him so I wouldn't have to sit my tender behind on the scratchy doormat.

Brick Glick's mother answered the door. His nice mother. She always gave me treats.

"Oh! Hello, Scratch, you adorable pug-faced, little bully-wooly, bulldog snookums."

That's me.

"Wait right here," she said, "and I'll get you a nice treat."

"But—" Flash said. He tapped his foot, waiting for her to come back.

My mouth became a waterfall of drool. Oh, boy. Oh, boy.

31

Mrs. Glick returned with a handful of doggie snacks. I gobbled one out of her hand, and she put the rest on the doorsill. Heaven, I love her!

"Now," she said, brushing off her hands, "what can I do for you, Mr. Fry with the silly green hat?"

"Is Brick home?"

"Brickford is still sleeping," she said. "But if you want him to come out and play with you, he can't. Not after what he did last night. Wait here, I'll wake him up."

"Oh, you don't have to—" Flash said, but Mrs. Glick was already gone. "Great, now he'll be mad and really turn us into frogs."

I licked the doggie snack crumbs off the doorsill. Even though I ate some dust, it was worth it.

Brick Glick stumbled to the door, and if I could laugh, I would have. The bully was wearing Smurf pajamas. Can you believe it? His hair was sticking out in every direction, his eyes were droopy and puffy, and he didn't look happy at all.

"You woke me up," Brick Glick said. "Why?"

I could see by the expression on Flash's face that he suddenly didn't know why the heck he came to see Brick Glick.

"Um, what'd you do last night?" Flash asked.

"You don't know? Seems everybody else in the world does."

"Know what?"

"None of your business!" Brick said. "Get out of here, or I'll turn you and the whole neighborhood into mushrooms."

Mrs. Glick appeared behind Brick. "Is that any way to talk to your friends?" Mrs. Glick spoke to Flash. "We had a call from Mrs. Hurthwurst this morning, Pete's mother. It seems that my son, here, threw some kind of firework at their house last night and shattered Pete's bedroom window. Brickford won't tell me a thing. Maybe he'll tell you why he did such a horrible thing."

"Aw, Mom," Brick moaned. Mrs. Glick turned and left.

"The rat," Brick said. "I'll get Pete for ratting on me."

Flash was so nervous he couldn't stop smiling.

"Are you laughing at me?" Brick said.

Brick stepped off the doorsill toward Flash. When his foot hit the doormat, a loud sound came from his feet: *BOOOF!* Then a terrible-smelling green smoke burst up and all around him.

Brick Glick jumped back. *"Arrgg!"* He coughed and growled like I do. *"Grrrrrr."* Then he lifted the doormat and kicked a small black plastic bag off the porch. "A smoke bomb!" he said.

"A smoke bomb?" Flash said. "What's that doing there?"

Brick looked at Flash. "What? Are you stupid? You know why it's there, and I know why it's there. Pete put it there to get back at me for my little firework last night."

"Gee," Flash said, "maybe he did. Why did you explode that firework last night?"

"I'll tell you why!" Brick roared. "I knew his slimy little sister stole my magic book, the book you still have and I'll still get."

"Marybeth stole it?" Flash said. "Really?"

"Yes! And I had to get back at her, so I thought I'd scare her a little with a harmless little firework. But I got Pete's room by mistake. So now Pete's getting back at me. The jerk is sticking up for his sister."

"Boy," Flash said, "you really goofed, huh?"

"I never goof!" Brick was trying to be scary, but he just looked silly in his pajamas, with hair sticking out and everything. Brick pointed a finger at Flash. "I'm telling you, Flash Fry-ball, and you can tell Pete—this means *war!*"

"Hold it, hold it, calm down," Flash said, gulping between each word. "You can't really blame Pete. I mean, it was Marybeth who stole your book, and it was Marybeth who made up that whole story about Pete missing and everything."

"So it *was* Marybeth," Brick said. "But I don't care. It was Pete who put this stinking smoke bomb here, and it is Pete who I will fight! Warn the world, Flash Fry. Brick Glick has declared war!"

"Wait a minute—" Flash said.

"And I want my magic book back. Now!"

Flash shook his head. "No, I won't give it to you. You'll only use it to attack Pete some more. Forget it."

Brick shook his head. "I'll never forget." Then he yawned and scratched his head. "I need my rest for the battle. Get out of here. And don't try to stop me."

Brick Glick stepped back, slammed the door, and all was silent.

I hunted for a few stray doggie treat crumbs, then followed Flash back into the street.

Things were getting dangerous. And I had a feeling that Flash wasn't going to make things any better.

When we finally got back home, someone was waiting for us. And that someone was very scared.

Eight: More War!

"Pete!" Flash said. "What are you doing here?"

Pete looked shaky and nervous. "I have to talk with you."

"Sure," Flash said, acting like a stupid bigshot. "Step down into my office."

Pete shook his head. "No. Your mother will hear us. Let's sit out in the backyard."

"Fine with me."

Pete and Flash sat on the long, wooden porch swing that was under a tree behind Flash's house. There was just enough room beside Flash for a dog. I hopped up and curled beside Flash. We began to swing as they began to talk.

"You're not going to believe what Brick Glick did last night," Pete said.

Flash held up his hand. "Say no more. I already know about the explosion. I just came back from Brick Glick's house."

"You did?"

"Sure I did. You're talking to Flash Fry, Private Eye. I'm one step ahead of everybody. Know what just happened at Brick's?"

Pete shook his head. "What?"

"Poof!" Flash said. "He stepped on a smoke bomb that was hidden under his doormat."

A small laugh popped from Pete's lips. "Really? What did he do?"

Flash began laughing, too. "He almost jumped out of his Smurf pajamas!"

The two guys laughed so hard that the rocking almost knocked me off the swing.

"Does he know who put it there?" Pete asked.

"Sure he does. You did."

"What!" Pete stopped laughing immediately. "I didn't put any smoke bomb on his porch."

"You don't have to lie to me, Pete," Flash said. "You're asking for big trouble, you know."

"Honest, I didn't put that smoke bomb there. You think I want to get Brick Glick angry? No way."

"Well, it doesn't matter, Pete. Brick blames you for it. In fact, he's declared war on you."

"War!"

"Yup. He says Marybeth stole his magic book. So, to get back at her, he exploded that firework last night—but he got your room by mistake. Now he blames you for sticking up for Marybeth and striking back with the smoke bomb. He says this means war."

Pete stopped swinging. "Terrific. But I don't care who stole his dumb book or put the smoke bomb on his porch. All I know is that first he gets Marybeth crying her head off at his house, and now he attacks our house—and my room—scaring my whole family out of our brains. I've had it with him."

"Yeah, but do you really want to fight him?"

Pete wasn't listening. He was getting madder and madder.

"Okay! All right!" Pete said. He jumped off the swing. "If it's war Brick wants, it's war he'll get. Tell him I'm declaring war, too!"

"Hold it, Pete. Think a minute."

"No! I'm sick of Brick's tricks and how he bullies my sister and how he blames me for everything. It's war, Fry. My tricks against his magic. And I mean it!"

With that, Pete stormed off and disappeared into the bushes.

"War. Great. Just great," Flash said. He rubbed me behind the ears. "What now, Scratch? Somehow I think I'm to blame for starting this whole mess. Gee, if I could only find Marybeth. Maybe I could give her Brick's magic book. Maybe if she returned it, and Brick and Marybeth apologized to each other, this whole thing would end. Hey! Yeah! That's the answer!"

Me, I didn't think that was a very good answer. But, heck, it was something to do.

Flash loaded me up in his bike's basket. For about an hour, we rode around the whole neighborhood, looking for Marybeth. She wasn't home, and no one we asked had seen her. Then, completely by accident, we found her in the strangest place.

36

Nine: The Meanest Girl in Town

Shun-chug, shun-chug, shun-chug...

The washing machines in the laundromat were churning away. My nose went crazy trying to smell all the soapy, sweaty, dirty, and hot smells floating around inside. Three women and two men were sitting in a row, reading magazines, waiting for their washes to get done. And over in the corner were two girls. A tall girl was loading her wash into a dryer, chatting with the other girl. The other girl was Marybeth.

Flash walked right up to her.

"So, here you are!" Flash said.

Marybeth's eyes popped out when she saw him. "How'd you find me?"

"Doesn't matter," Flash said. "I have to talk to you."

The other girl took one look at Flash and laughed. "What the heck are you wearing that big green hat for?"

"He's a detective, Patty," Marybeth said.

The girl rolled her eyes. "Sure he is."

"This is serious," Flash said to Marybeth. "Your brother's in big trouble. Come outside and let's chat."

I almost laughed. I couldn't believe Flash had actually said, "Let's chat." Geesh.

"Oh, all right," Marybeth said. "Be right back, Patty."

The three of us walked outside. Now I knew why Marybeth had smelled of Rainbow detergent when we first met her—now she reeked of it. I sniffed around the bottom of a garbage can for goodies, found nothing, then curled up on a sunny patch of soap-smelling grass. Flash and Marybeth sat on a bench, facing the main street of town. A huge truck roared by, and Flash waited until the noise went away before he spoke.

"Brick Glick and Pete have declared war on each other."

This took Marybeth by surprise. "What!"

"It's true. I heard about that explosion last night. Here's what else happened." Flash told her all about the smoke bomb and his talks with Brick and Pete.

When Flash was done, all Marybeth did was laugh one short laugh. "Who cares? Not me. Pete has been playing practical jokes on me all my life. Who cares if he fights Brick? I'm glad they're fighting. Finally, I'm getting back at my brother."

I hadn't seen this mean streak in Marybeth before. But I sure was seeing it now. It took Flash by surprise, too.

"What do you mean, you're getting back at him?" Flash asked.

"You sure are slow, Flash. Yes, sure, I made up the story about Pete being missing. I wanted to get Pete in trouble with Brick. How? I stole Brick's magic book. I left the book and one of Pete's rubber horseflies down by the pond so you'd find it, tell Brick, and Brick would think Pete stole his book. And when Brick attacked our house last night and broke Pete's window, that was the best thing that could have happened. I had a real chance to get Brick mad at my nerdy brother. That's why I put the smoke bomb under Brick's doormat."

"*You* put it there?" Flash said.

Even I was surprised at that one. I growled and shook my head.

"Sure I did," Marybeth said, very proud of herself. "I knew Brick would think Pete put it there, and I was right, right?"

"Right. Brick blames Pete for the smoke bomb, and Pete blames Brick for the explosion. And now there's a big war, all because of your lies and stupid tricks."

Marybeth laughed. "This is great! It worked!"

"Listen to me, Marybeth. You know how mean Brick can get. Your brother could really get hurt sticking up for you, don't you understand that? Pete really likes you and feels sorry for you because Brick made you cry. How can you do this to him?"

"Easy," she said.

Boy, was she mean.

"You have to help me stop them, Marybeth. Right now, I'll bet Brick is getting all his magic together and Pete is getting all his tricks together to have one gigantic war. You can stop it, if you want to."

"Well, I don't want to. Besides, I don't think they'll really fight. Brick only sneaks around at night, and Pete only plays his jokes on little girls like me. Neither of them is brave enough to face the other in the daytime."

"But, if they do, it'll all be your fault."

Marybeth stood up. "This is boring. Sorry, I can't help you, Flash. See ya." And Marybeth went back into the laundromat.

"What a creep," Flash said. I rubbed up against his leg so he knew I agreed with him.

But Flash wasn't giving up. He hid around the corner of the building and waited. Soon Marybeth and Patty were done with the laundry. Patty called her mother, who came in a small red car and picked her up. Marybeth started walking home, and Flash and I snuck along behind her, hiding behind bushes and trees.

Suddenly, we heard a loud *ZZZZZZZZZZZZZING!* Up ahead, something flew through air over the trees, spreading little silver snippets of foil that floated down to earth. Underneath these small pieces of foil was Pete.

Marybeth hid behind a fence, and we ducked behind a bush. Pete threw something back that was red and round. It soared over a hedge and landed three feet from Brick Glick. The red thing burst with a great gush of water. A water balloon. And Brick was soaked. Brick shouted something, then raced after Pete. Both of them disappeared.

"The war has begun," Flash said. He rose and ran up to Marybeth. "Did you see that? Did you?"

"You were following me!" she said.

"Did you see that?" Flash said. "War! I told you. You said they wouldn't fight, and they are. It's started already."

Marybeth shrugged. "I was wrong. Big deal."

"It is a big deal," Flash said. "You're to blame for this. We have to do something."

"Maybe," she said.

"Not maybe. We *have* to stop them. Brick is so stubborn he'll never give up. Do you want Brick attacking your house again? Maybe *your* room this time? Huh?"

"Of course not," Marybeth said.

"Okay, here's the plan," Flash said. "Uh. Ummm. Let me think a minute."

Not too quick, is he?

"Got it! Marybeth, you go find Pete. Talk to him. Get him to stop fighting with Brick. I don't care how you do it. Lie to him. You're good at lies. Tell him that someone called the cops.

Yeah, tell him the cops are after him and Brick. That'll get him to stop quick." Flash thought some more. "And I'll go after Brick and try to talk him out of it, too. I'll call you later to see how you did. Or you call me. Okay?"

"Sure, sure," Marybeth said. And she wandered off.

I didn't believe that Marybeth was going to do anything. I think she just agreed to the whole thing to get Flash off her back.

"Come on, Scratch," Flash said. "I promised Mom I'd be home for lunch. Let's go eat, then find Brick Glick. I have a surefire way of stopping him from fighting. I'll tell him that if he doesn't stop, I'll rip his magic book to shreds! Let's go!"

Not a bad idea, I thought. But then all I was thinking about was food. I beat Flash home by about five minutes.

Ten: A Mad Magician

Most dogs get fed twice a day. Not me. After years of prancing around, drooling a lot, and getting the family to feel really sorry for me, I'd trained them into giving me three meals a day. It's great. Soon I'll start training them for a fourth meal.

I dove into my chicken liver dog food—my favorite flavor—and Flash sat up at the table with his Mom and a peanut-butter-and-strawberry-jelly sandwich with a banana on the side.

"What are you up to today?" Flash's Mom asked, taking a spoonful of her cottage cheese. Yuk.

"Oh, nothing much."

"Catching any gangsters or criminals?"

Flash blushed. "No."

Flash's mom always made fun of Flash's detective business, and Flash didn't like it. She didn't know that Flash wasn't just playing around—he was a detective for real. Flash changed the subject quickly.

"Gotta go," he said.

"Not so fast, young man. There are some chores to do."

"Aw, Mom. I'll do them later, I promise. I've got something really important I have to do."

"You can play after you finish your chores."

"Honest, Mom, this can't wait."

His mom sighed and shook her head. "What is it this time? A bank robber? A kidnapping?"

Flash looked his mother in the eye and said, "A war."

She pretended to be concerned. "Oh, a war. Well, now, that's more important than any old bank robber, isn't it? Why didn't you tell me it was a war before? Certainly, you can do your chores later. But don't forget."

Flash wiped his mouth, rose, and adjusted his wide-brimmed

green hat on his head. "Thanks, Mom. See ya later. Let's go, Scratch."

We hustled outside.

"Now, down to business. We have to find Brick and stop this war. Here's the plan."

The plan was simple: We'd ask everyone we saw in the neighborhood if they'd seen Brick Glick. If anyone didn't want to talk, I decided I'd give them my mad-dog act and scare them into talking.

First, we checked Brick's house to see if he was there. Nope. Then Flash and I started down Bain Street, looking for likely people to question. The first person Flash decided to question was about four years old. He was a bright-eyed kid on a shiny new tricycle.

"Hi," Flash said.

The kid pointed to me. "You've got a doggie!"

"That's right," Flash said. "He's a nice doggie, too. Aren't you, Scratch?"

Yeah, sure, I'm a great doggie. I went over and licked the kid's hand to show him how nice I was. He giggled and couldn't stop looking where I licked him.

"What color is my hat?" Flash asked.

The kid thought a moment. "Green?"

"That's right! And what color is Scratch's nose?"

The kid put his hand over his mouth and giggled. "Black."

"Right again! Black. Have you ever seen anyone dressed in black clothes?"

The boy nodded eleven times. "Yes. Dracula, the vampire."

"No, no, I mean have you seen him around here. Walking down the street."

The boy thought that over for a minute. Then his eyes got wide, and his big mouth screamed. "Dracula is *here?* He's on my *street?*"

"No, no, that's not—"

The kid leaped off his tricycle and ran crying toward the house. "Mommy! Mommy! Dracula's here! Dracula's here!"

I thought Flash's questioning was pretty smart. Too bad.

We continued walking.

Then Flash suddenly stopped. He was staring across the street. I stared, too.

There, walking with their mother, were Johnny and George Jones, the two kids Flash had read about in the newspaper—

43

the kids who were chased out of the spooky old Doomer house by, gulp, zombies.

I could tell that the kids were still scared by the way they stuck really close to their mom and by the way their eyes were bugged out.

"Poor kids," Flash said. "I wonder what they really saw in that house? Hope I never find out."

Me, either.

"Let's go."

We questioned a few more people but got nowhere. A little while later, Flash saw a man mowing his lawn over to the left, and we headed that way.

"Excuse me," Flash said to the man, shouting over the roar of the lawn mower's engine. "Do you know Brick Glick?"

"The kid's a creep!" the man with the lawn mower said. He was a thick-necked man with huge hands. "The blasted kid just ran through my flowerbed not twenty minutes ago, chasing that Hurthwurst brat!"

"Really?"

"You calling me a liar?"

"No, I just—"

"Let them kill each other, I say. Who gives a blasted rusty penny? The whole blasted town would jump up and down and cheer! I'm sick of the blasted two of them, hear me? Sick!"

Flash had sense enough to retreat. "Well, um, thanks a lot."

The man roared off, pushing his lawn mower and spewing grass. It smelled great. I ate some until he yelled at me.

"So the war is going full blast," Flash said. "Come on, Scratch, maybe we can catch up with them."

As we walked, I felt and sniffed and tasted the breeze. It was going to rain, and rain hard. Probably a thunderstorm. I knew it would start raining around nightfall. Dogs sense these things. I can feel the electricity in the air and smell the fresh, crisp stormfront sneaking in. Dogs are great at this, better than human weathermen. Someday—mark my words —you'll turn on your TV news program to watch the weather-dog.

We didn't have to walk too far. We went through a couple of backyards and soon found ourselves in the huge city park. There, out in the middle of the baseball field, standing right on top of the pitcher's mound, was Brick Glick. He was just

44

standing there with hands on his hips, looking around. His back was to us, so he didn't hear us come up behind him.

"Brick," Flash said.

Brick jumped and stumbled back. The ends of his long sleeves fell over his knuckles. What a character.

"Fry. Whew, you scared me a little. You never know what I'm going to do if you take me by surprise. I might accidentally turn you into a lollipop or something."

"Sure, Brick, sure," Flash said. "What are you doing out here?"

"I had Pete on the run, then lost him. Don't know where he went. But mark my words, there will be a showdown soon. I guarantee it. In fact, we've already arranged it."

"A showdown?"

"Yes. What's a war without a showdown? But that's all I'm telling you, because I want you to butt out, Fry. Get it?"

"Sorry, but I'm butting in," Flash said. Boy, is he brave. "I want you to stop this war. Now."

"Forget it," Brick Glick said, waving his hand and his sleeve. "It's too late now. And, by the way, I want my magic book back."

"You want it for the showdown, right?"

"Bingo."

"Forget it," Flash said. "I'll give you the book if you stop this war."

Brick thought a moment. "Okay, it's a deal. Gimme the book."

"Hold on a second," Flash said. "I don't trust you. No, you stop the war first, then I'll give you the book, maybe in a week or so."

Brick snapped his fingers. "Darn. Almost had you. No deal, then. The war is on."

"Let's put it this way," Flash said all cockylike. "If you don't stop this war, I'll rip your magic book to shreds!"

Brick Glick's face turned bright red. "You do that, and I'll declare war on *you!*"

That was something Flash didn't expect. Flash gulped and turned red himself.

"Are you going to give me my book?" Brick asked.

"No," Flash said. "Are you going to stop this war?"

"No," Brick said.

They stared at each other a minute.

"Then we have nothing more to talk about," Brick said. And he walked away.

"But—and—ummm," Flash said, watching the black figure of Brick disappear between two houses. "Boy, I guess I goofed that one up."

Now we were the ones standing alone on the pitcher's mound.

"Well," Flash sighed, "guess I might as well go home and do my chores while I figure out what to do next. I'll call Marybeth, too, to see if she's talked to Pete yet."

We headed home. And, a little while after we got there, we discovered a couple of things that would keep us up way into the dark, rainy night.

Eleven: Gone! Gone! Gone! Gone!

"Hello! You down there, kid-o?" It was Flash's mother, hollering down the basement steps from the kitchen.

"Yeah, I'm here," Flash yelled back.

"Ready to do those chores?"

"Okay. Be right up," Flash said.

The chores he was supposed to do were the usual ones. Empty all the garbage cans in the house, pick up anything I might have left behind in the backyard grass, and clean his room. But, before he went up to do them, he stood there thinking a minute.

Me, I stood there whining because I knew what he was about to discover. And it wasn't good.

Flash turned and walked over behind his desk.

There, on the shelf, was nothing.

"The magic book's gone!"

Flash bolted upstairs, screaming, "Mom! Mom!" I heard him ask her if anyone else came into the basement while he was out. She said of course not.

But someone *had* been there. The magic book was gone.

"Had to be Brick Glick," Flash said. "He probably left the ballfield and came right over here and swiped it. Terrific."

He thought for a second, then lunged for the phone and dialed.

"Hello, is Marybeth there?"

I could hear the butler's voice say, "No, sorry."

"Well, is Pete there?"

Another no.

Flash thanked him and hung up.

"Where is everybody?" Flash wondered. Then he wondered some more. "Wonder what Brick meant by a showdown?

Hmmm. I'm sure Pete could tell me, if I could find him. Maybe I should go out and—"

"Hello, down there, again!" Flash's Mom hollered. "Where are you? Let's get at those chores, huh?"

"I'm coming, I'm coming," Flash said. "I'm never going to solve this case." He laid his big green hat on his desk and tromped upstairs.

Me, I had an idea. I bolted out of the house.

I was heading for an old pal of mine, Marzipan. She's a frisky and friendly Irish Setter. We'd almost fallen in love once, but the human she lives with fenced in their yard, and now she doesn't get out at all. She was looking through the squares of the wire fence at me, swishing her beautiful long tail and stomping her two front feet, which told me to come over. I went over.

I leaned in, and she licked my nose through the fence. I licked hers. We both pranced a little, sniffing. Then I sat on the other side of the fence to talk with her. It reminded me of those prison movies where someone comes to visit a convict and they have to talk through the wire mesh.

I raised both eyebrows and tilted my head. She stuck out her left foot, sat down, got up, turned sideways, and hung out her tongue. Wow. She just told me she missed me. My heart began to thump.

We talked some more, using the silent language I told you about before. Here's a translation:

"You never come to visit," Marzipan said.

"I've been busy."

"The same old Scratch. Always too busy. You're the free one. I'm caged up, remember? The least you could do is run over once in a while."

"We had some great times, didn't we?"

Marzipan nodded her eyes. "Yes, we did. But now I'm stuck in this yard. Oh, it's so boring sometimes."

"I know what you mean."

We sat there and just looked at each other for a moment. I couldn't keep my eyes off her long red hair and cute wet nose. Gorgeous.

"Flash and I are on a case," I finally said.

"Really? How exciting! Can I help? I'd love to help. I've got nothing to do in here."

48

"Sure, you can help. Do you know Brick Glick?"

She turned and ran into the center of her yard. She spun in two circles, barking four times. She was mad. Then she trotted back.

"Yes," she said, "I know him. He's mean. He throws rocks at me that explode. If I could get out of here, I'd take a big taste of him."

"Know what you mean. Have you seen him around in the past hour or so?"

"Yes, I did. I saw Brick running into the woods with a bag full of his awful tricks. He scares me, Scratch. I wish you were around to protect me from him."

"Me, too."

"I saw someone else, too, Scratchie, if it will help."

"Who?"

"I know this boy, because he is always nice to me. He pets me and throws sticks for me to chase. He's a nice boy who—"

"Who was it? Who was it?"

"Pete What's-his-name. He was running, too—everybody is running into the woods. Pete was carrying some kind of big sack with him. I don't know what was in it."

I had a feeling that all his tricks were in that bag. I also had a feeling that they were both running into the woods for a good reason. Showdown!

"Thanks for the information, Marz," I said.

We licked each other's noses again.

"It's going to thunder and lightning and rain soon. In two hours, I think, at dark."

"I know," I said.

A big, round, human head with a beard on the bottom stuck out the back door of Marzipan's house. "Marzipan! Bath time! Here girl! Come on!"

"Bath time," she said. "Oh, boy. He found a flea in the house and blames me. The flea was never on me, Scratch. It hopped a ride into the house on his sock. How can you tell humans that? What's a dog to do?"

"Take a bath, I guess," I said. "Look, I gotta be hustling along, Marz. Big case. Very big. You've really helped."

She laughed. "Good. Come back soon, please?"

"I promise."

"We had some good times, didn't we, Scratch?"

"We sure did."

We licked noses again, and she ran toward the house. I sat and watched her until she was inside.

Those kids are having their showdown somewhere in the woods, but how do I tell Flash what I know? Somehow I had to get him into the woods to investigate. But now it was almost suppertime, and Flash's parents won't let him do anything until after he eats. Food first.

I raced home.

Twelve: A Holler for Help

After Flash had finished his chores, his Mom made him stay inside to peel some carrots and potatoes to help her get dinner ready. So the next couple of hours were pretty boring. It started to get dark soon, and just as I said, thunder began to rattle the windows, and rain began to pour down. I just lay around, trying to figure out some way to tell Flash what I knew. But, as things turned out, he found out about most of it.

I got up and took a few laps from my dusty water bowl. What I really wished I could do was open the refrigerator and pop open a cold bottle of soda. Maybe have a pretzel or two, maybe some onion dip. Or maybe take a few huge, mouth-watering bites out of that delicious roast beef that Flash's mom was taking out of the oven. The wonderful smell of it made me whine. And maybe I might like some of those carrots and mashed potatoes that Flash's dad was spooning into serving bowls. Mmmmm. Yummy.

So I sat there with my tongue lolling out, making sad eyes at the terrific human food, sniffing like crazy to inhale all the good fumes I could, and waiting for someone to fill my bowl on the floor.

Flash soon opened a can of Wonderdog with the electric can opener. After smelling the delicious roast beef, the wet, gloppy Wonderdog smelled like bad breath. I began eating my food like a dog.

"I wonder if Marybeth talked Pete out of the war," Flash said to himself. "Why hasn't she called?" He went to the table to eat.

Just when I was done eating, the phone rang. Flash's father answered it and said it was for Flash. Flash got on the phone, and I wandered down and flopped at his feet to listen with my super ears.

51

"Hello?" Flash said.

"It's me," the voice said. "Pete. I'm in a phone booth. No time to talk. I need your help, bad. In big trouble, Flash, big trouble."

"What?" Flash said. "Talk, Pete. Brick said you two are having a showdown tonight. Didn't Marybeth talk to you?"

Pete didn't answer the question. "I'm really scared, Flash. You have to stop Brick! I thought he was only kidding about all the war stuff, but he's serious! I don't want to meet Brick, but now I have no choice."

"Now everybody's fighting!" Flash said. "Where is it happening? Tell me, and I'll be there. I'll go with you."

"Great! Thanks, Flash. It's at the house in— Oh, no!" Pete screamed. Then the phone clicked. Silence buzzed from Pete's end.

Flash hung up. "Pete's in trouble. The tricks showdown is on," he said in a whisper. "But where? In a house. There are hundreds of houses around here! If I don't find out which one, I can't do anything!"

I growled. Why did I growl? Because I was mad. Why was I mad? Because I couldn't talk—and I was dying to tell Flash that I knew which house Pete meant! There was only one house it could be, and the house was in the woods. I had to get Flash into the woods in the pouring rain and thunder and lightning—before it was too late!

Thirteen: Running in the Rain

Flash was at the table, finishing up his strawberry shortcake, so I had to wait. Why does he have to eat slowly now?

When he was done, he burped and got yelled at. Then he walked over to the window and pulled aside the curtain. It was dark out and raining steadily and hard. Lightning slashed and flashed, and thunder exploded like cannons. I was barking like bullets.

"*Shhhh,* Scratch. What should I do? Brick and Pete are going to have their showdown any minute, and I don't know where."

I do! I do! I galloped around the chair. I stopped in front of him and whined and panted and crossed my back legs.

"Have you got to go out?" he asked. "Now? In the rain?"

You bet I have to go out. And you don't know it yet, but you're coming with me.

"All right, allll right."

I danced for joy and ran down into the basement. He always lets me out through the basement doors. He plodded slowly down the stairs after me, taking them one by one.

I clawed on the basement doors, whining and yipping.

Faster! We have to hurry!

Flash opened the basement doors. "Don't get too wet," he called after me.

I sprang out into the darkness and rain. It felt great, and it made me have to go. I went. Then I looked back to Flash. He was leaning against the door, scratching his head.

How do I get him outside? Then how do I get him to follow me?

I barked at him.

He waved. Great.

Then I had an idea.

53

I walked back toward him, pretending to come in. Then I made believe I heard something behind me, a noise in the backyard. I whirled around and barked my throat out.

"What is it, boy?" Flash said. "See something out there?"

I looked back at him with a wild look in my eyes, then turned and barked again into the darkness.

"What do you see, Scratch?"

I barked a few more times, then bolted into the backyard like I was chasing something. I ran around a bush and hid, watching what Flash would do.

He was putting on his yellow rubber raincoat with the silly hood. He grabbed his flashlight and came out into the rain. The beam of light from the flashlight shot through the dark like a laser beam, lighting up the raindrops like falling diamonds.

"Scratch? Where are you, boy? What'd you find?"

I took off from behind the bush, barking loudly so he knew where I was. I headed into the woods, and Flash was running right behind me like a good boy.

It worked.

I stopped every now and then, pretending to sniff a trail, but actually I was giving him time to catch his breath. I was also trying to listen through the rain. Up ahead, I heard what I hoped I would hear. When he was ready, I took off again, deeper into the woods.

"Hey!" Flash yelled. "Wait up! Where are you going?"

Thunder thundered, and lightning lit above the treetops as we tromped and splashed over the muddy ground.

Soon we were just where I wanted us to be. At the treehouse. I stopped and barked up toward the treehouse.

"What are you barking at, boy? A cat? Is a cat up there, boy?"

Then we heard two screams from the treehouse.

"Help! Help!"

"It's those two kids!" Flash said. He cupped a hand around his mouth and called, "Hey! Kids! Come on down! There's lightning!"

"We can't!" the boy yelled. "The rain came! The ladder fell! We're trapped forever!"

A huge roll of thunder seemed to pass through the trees. The two kids started crying and screaming and kicking up one heck of a fuss.

"Stay there!" Flash said. "I'll come up and get you."

Flash stuck the flashlight in his pocket, picked up the ladder, placed it against the tree trunk, then climbed up to the door that was cut in the bottom of the treehouse. He helped the little girl down the ladder, then the little boy. Then Flash came down and stood beside them, sheltering them with his raincoat. Me, I was soaked.

"It's you!" the boy said to Flash.

"Huh?" Flash said.

"We didn't mean it! We didn't mean it!"

"Mean what?"

"It was *his* idea not to tell you!" the girl said, pointing at the boy. "It was *his* idea not to tell you anything about the girl at the pond. It was *his* idea to stay here till dark. *He* said the rain would stop right away! But it di-di-didn't!"

Flash looked at the boy. "You knew stuff and didn't tell me, even when we asked you this morning?"

"Yes," the wet boy said. He was proud of that.

"Just now," the girl shouted over the roar of the rain, "Brick and that other boy were throwing fire at each other *right by our tree!* We were too sc-scared to leave, because the two wizards might see us! Then the ladder fell down! Then it was raining hard, and *we couldn't go home!*"

"Where'd they go?" Flash asked the boy.

"I'm not telling," the boy said. He crossed his arms.

"You tell me," said Flash, "or I'll put you back up in that treehouse."

Fear turned the boy's eyes into fried eggs. "They're in the ghost house! In the ghost house!"

Thunder shook the ground.

The little girl screamed. "Please, don't put us back in the tree castle!"

The tree castle. How cute.

"Please!" the boy added.

Before we could stop them, the boy took the girl's hand, and they ran away into the night. Up ahead, I could hear their father calling for them. They'd be okay.

Now it was up to Flash to figure it out. I waited, tasting raindrops on my tongue. If he didn't figure out which house the kids meant pretty soon, I'd start my chasing act again.

"Kids," Flash said, shaking his head. "Ghost house. Ha!"

I was just about to grab his raincoat in my teeth and drag

him with me when another thought hit him. It's usually his second thoughts that are the best.

"But wait," he said. "There *is* a ghost house around here. The old Doomer place. I read about it in the paper yesterday. It's empty and crumbling, and everybody says it's haunted. Yeah! And Pete said they were going to a house! That's where Pete and Brick are fighting tonight! We'd better hurry! Come on, Scratch, what are you just sitting there for?"

Fourteen: Wails of Welcome

It began to rain even harder. I led the way with my nose, and Flash followed with the flashlight. I could tell he was scared by the way he kept swallowing and by the way the beam of light bounced all over the place.

The old, creepy Doomer house. Empty. Falling apart. Haunted.

I couldn't help thinking about Johnny and George Jones. They're probably scared for life because of what they saw in this house. And we were about to go inside.

And there it was.

We could just see it through the thick web of tangled, wet branches. It was worse than anybody ever said it was.

The house sat there in the rain like a huge toad. Its high, pointed roof was surrounded by swirling fog. The outside of the place had been white once, but now it was all rotten and almost black. All the windows were broken, and vines were growing up the peeling outside walls like grasping hands of some horrible monster. There was no light in any of the windows. It was black-hole dark. The entire house leaned a little bit to the left, almost as if it were listening to something.

I began to whine, and Flash stroked my dripping fur with his shaking hand. Lightning crackled, and we both jumped. Then thunder barked, and we jumped again.

"What if they're not in there?" Flash whispered.

Me, I kind of hoped they weren't.

But they were, because right then, through the steady chatter of the rain, we heard a faint scream come from inside the old Doomer house.

"*Aaaaaaaaaa . . .*"

"Who was that?" Flash whispered. "Come on, there's no time to lose."

We began to shove our way through the sharp, thorny bushes. They grabbed at my fur and poked into my ribs. I growled and kept going. No branch was going to scare me.

Flash aimed the flashlight at the front of the house. A slimy rat scurried off the porch. Its tiny eyes gleamed at us from under a bush.

We didn't see anyone, or hear anything else. Even I didn't hear anything except the fast plippity-plop of the rain.

Side by side, we headed toward the porch. The warped floorboards dipped and rose like frozen waves.

Flash patted me on the head. "It's only a house. That's all."

Sure it is, I thought. Like King Kong is only a monkey.

We carefully walked up to the top of the steps. I shook the water off my bod. Flash flipped back his hood. Then we both stared at the tall front door.

"Maybe it's locked," Flash said.

He took three steps to the door.

"Yaaaaaa-yaaaaa-raaaaaaaaaaaaaaaa!" An ear-splitting scream cut through the night, and we both jumped back.

"Wha-what was that?" Flash said.

Well, it wasn't me, that's for sure.

"Whatever it is," Flash said, "it's gone now. Come on, Scratch, we've gotta do what we've gotta do."

Flash stepped up to the door again.

"Yaaaaa-yaaaaaa-raaaaaaaaaaaaaaaaaa!"

We leaped back with a scream of our own.

Then I thought I'd try something.

I walked up to the door.

"Yaaaaaa!"

I quickly stepped back.

I walked up.

"Raaaaaaa!"

I stepped back.

"Hey," Flash said.

Flash squatted down and lifted a corner of the moldy door-mat in front of the front door. Beneath the mat was something that looked like a small, black hot water bottle. Flash picked it up with two fingers.

He squeezed the black thing.

"Yaaaaaa!"

"A scream cushion!" Flash said. "It's only a gag! Pete has to be inside! Come on!"

Flash tossed the scream cushion aside and reached for the doorknob. But, before he could grab it, the door began to creak open all by itself.

Flash and I whined together.

The door opened all the way and stopped.

"The wind," Flash said.

Sure.

Fifteen: Room of Doom

"I wonder if we'll see any zombies," Flash said.

Flash and I gulped, and very carefully we entered the spooky, dark Doomer house. Right away I began sniffing to see who or what I could smell, but all I snorted into my nose was dust.

"Zzzzooof!" I sneezed.

Flash jumped about three feet to his right. "Cut that out!" he whispered.

He closed the door. Flash's face was as white as milk as he shined the flashlight all over the place. I got glimpses of big dusty rooms, lots of moldy wood, cobwebs, broken glass sprinkled on the floor, and plaster peeling off the ceilings like flaps of skin.

Once upon a time, this house must have looked wonderful. People and dogs lived here and laughed and played and danced and had babies and maybe even ate some pizza. Now only three things lived here: spiders, rats, and . . . ghosts. What do I do if I meet a ghost? Bite it? I didn't think that would work. I didn't think my mad-dog act would work, either, whether or not I foamed at the mouth. Running, that would work. Folks, I was scared.

Suddenly, from seemingly everywhere, we heard a voice.

"Go away, Fry, or you and your poochie will end up as cockroaches!"

"Brick Glick," Flash whispered.

"Helllllllllp!" another voice echoed from somewhere in the house.

"Pete!" Flash said.

Footsteps ran away into the darkness. Then the entire house was filled with the laughter of Brick Glick.

"Brick must have done something to Pete," Flash said.

"Their war is going strong. I—I—I guess we have to go upstairs."

I was listening hard. But with the rain echoing all over the place, I couldn't hear anyone. If anybody was near us, he or she had to be floating through the air. I wished I hadn't thought that.

"Come on," Flash said.

He aimed the flashlight at the staircase, and we followed the yellow beam up the stairs to the end of a long hallway. The place smelled like burning rubber. I felt like sneezing again, but held it in.

There were ten closed doors, five on each side. About halfway down the corridor was an ugly large black splotch that had eaten through the carpet and the rubber pad beneath. From the ragged rim of the carpet came thin streams of smoke that were snaking slowly upward.

"Brick and Pete must have just had a battle here," Flash whispered. He gulped loudly. "Come on. We have to look in those r-rooms."

He raised the flashlight, and we followed the beam down to the first door. Flash boldly put his hand on the first doorknob, turned it, then gave the door a good shove and stepped back. The door opened, and Flash's light showed us a small, harmless, empty room. We took a quick peek inside, then backed out.

"One down, nine to go," Flash said.

We moved to the second door. It was locked. We moved to the third. Locked. The fourth, fifth, sixth, seventh, eighth, and ninth doors were also locked.

"One door to go," he said. "A-And it's open."

Flash quickly slid around to the side of the door like a cop, then suddenly booted the door open with his foot. Nothing came leaping out at us. We waited a moment, then slowly entered the room. The window on the far side was broken, and the wet night wind was whistling in.

Before Flash had a chance to raise the flashlight, both of us began clawing at our faces. We had walked right into a gigantic spider web!

"*Uk, uk, uk, uk!*" Flash said, shivering with disgust.

Then the spiders attacked. Hundreds of them fell on top of us, and Flash let loose with a wild scream, flailing his arms and legs. My paws were going crazy, and my teeth snapped and bit at the crawling mass of disgusting bugs.

Then we both realized something at the same time.

"Hey!" Flash said. He was standing still now, shining the light on a spider that sat quietly in his palm. "They're rubber spiders!"

Sure enough, they were. Large, horrible, black rubber spiders with wiggly legs.

"It's a trick!" Flash said. "We stepped right into either Brick's or Pete's trap. Had to be Pete. It's his style." Flash was shivering. "Let's get out of here."

We walked back into the hall, brushing off all the phony spider web stuff we could.

I don't know about Flash, but I felt just a little bit braver now. So far we hadn't seen one real ghost. All we saw were tricks. And tricks can't hurt you. Can they?

Flash was cocky. "Gags. I say there's nothing to be afraid of in this big old house except silly jokes played by two dumb kids."

Then, without warning, *BAM!* The door to the tenth room quickly whooshed and slammed shut.

Flash and I flattened against the wall. Our yelps of terror were drowned out by a deep blast of thunder that rolled out and wrapped around the house.

"Th-that had to be the wind," Flash said. He moved to the door and turned the knob. He quickly jumped back.

The door was locked.

The wind doesn't lock doors.

Sixteen: A Ghost and a Gross-out

We clung so tightly to the wall that if anybody saw us, they'd swear we were some strange kind of wallpaper, or a picture of a boy and his dog about to go crazy.

"Had to be a trick, had to be," Flash kept saying over and over again.

Thunder rumbled.

I felt a faint gust of breeze and turned to my left. I saw that another staircase climbed up to a small landing, then turned left and out of sight. It was dark up there. Flash saw it at the same time I did. He lifted his flashlight and shot a golden beam up the stairs.

"Wuh!" he said.

"Roo?" I said.

There, hanging in midair over the landing, was something foggy and very white. It shimmered and shifted in the beam of the flashlight.

"Raaaaaaakkkk," it said with a breathless voice.

Then the ghost began to move.

"Mommy!" Flash screamed.

Oh, no, I thought, Flash has finally lost his mind. He thought the ghost was his mommy.

"Raaaaaakkk-kkk."

We stood there, frozen to the floor in fear, and watched as the ghost swayed back and forth and seemed to bulge in and out at its middle. We inhaled for about ten seconds.

Then we saw a face. Somebody dressed in black screamed and raced off to the right.

"Brick!" Flash yelled.

Flash took a running step, then his foot found a hole in the rotting carpet, and down he went. *CRASH!* The flashlight

flew from his hand and rolled about five feet away. It was still on and shined back in Flash's face.

I ran to him. I licked his nose and eyes. He'd be fine.

"Wonder what scared Brick?" Flash said.

Then we heard a noise.

thump

> *thump*

>> *thump*

Something was slowly coming down the stairs. It was too dark to see what it was, and I couldn't smell anything.

thump

> *thump*

>> *thump*

Lightning streaked past the window at the far end of the hall, and in that quick second of light, we saw what it was—

A hand. A bloody hand. Its pale fingers arched up and pulled it across the step until it flopped off the edge, then its fingers worked again until it reached the next step.

Flash leaped up and dove back onto his butt. I lunged over and grabbed the flashlight in my teeth, then brought it back to Flash.

The hand plopped off the last step and began crawling toward Flash. It made a wet, flapping sound.

Flash held out his arm and aimed the flashlight like it was a gun. The hand was even more horrible in the light.

I growled and slowly approached it. It kept crawling, ignoring me. I sniffed. Just as I thought. I grabbed the hand in my teeth. Its fingers were wiggling around my face.

"Put it *down!*" Flash yelled. "Down, boy! Put it down!"

I pranced over to Flash and dropped the hand in his lap.

Flash screamed.

He stopped screaming when he got a good look at the hand.

"Hey," Flash said. "It's rubber." Flash picked it up and tugged on one of the moving fingers. "It's a fake. Look, here's the place for the batteries. Pete's trick!"

Flash stood. He tossed the hand on the floor, where it hit with one flat smack and began to crawl away down the hall.

"I've had it," Flash said. "I'm not falling for any more

66

tricks. "Now I'm mad." He cupped his hands around his mouth and yelled. "Brick! Pete! I'm going to stop you if it's the last thing I do!"

From the distance came the hollow mocking laughter of Brick Glick.

"Come on, Scratch. Nothing can stop us now!"

His foot was hovering over the first step when the eerie tinkling music began.

Seventeen: A Bark in the Dark

My ears stood straight up.

Faint, high music was floating through the house. It was like Tinkerbell music—only scary.

"Has to be a trick," Flash said.

"What was that?" we heard Pete say from very far away.

Then we heard Brick answer him: *"I—I d-don't know! It wasn't me!"*

"It wasn't me, either!"

If it was a trick, I thought, who played it? Not Pete. Not Brick. Then who...or *what?*

Flash started climbing the stairs. I followed. We reached the landing and took a left. Another short set of stairs led us to a door. Immediately, I started barking.

"What is it, boy?" Flash said.

I scratched on the door, throwing in some whines and a couple of more barks.

"Hear something, Scratch?"

Flash got the message. He turned the doorknob and opened the door. The huge room must have once been a library. Empty, dusty shelves lined every wall. Rain spat in through the large, broken windows.

In the center of the room was Brick Glick. Up against the far wall was Pete, with his arms over his head. Brick reached into his bag, and suddenly he was holding a large handful of stinking black mud.

"Take that!" he screamed. He whipped back around and threw the mud at Pete. Pete's eyes grew wide, and he ran to the right. The mud flopped against the wall and slid to the floor. Pete ran out through another door.

"I'll get you yet!" Brick yelled after Pete.

Flash sneezed.

Brick whirled around and smiled at Flash. "There you are!" Brick got his hand all tangled up in the straps of his bag of magic. Then his hand disappeared inside and came out with a water pistol.

"A water pistol?" Flash said. "You're gonna shoot us with a water pistol?"

Brick squeezed the trigger. A burst of blue stuff shot out and splattered on Flash's right leg.

"Paint!" Flash said. "Hey, cut that out!"

"Unless you want me to turn you into blue boy and your mutt into blue dog, you'll do as I say. Move!" Brick motioned with his head to the left. We shuffled to the left.

"What are you going to do?" Flash asked.

"Open that door!" Brick Glick said.

Flash looked down and saw a doorknob. He opened the door. "Get in," Brick said.

Flash's mouth fell open. "But it's a closet!"

Brick aimed the paint pistol at Flash's face. "Sorry, Fry, but I can't have you getting in my way. Inside, if you please—unless you and your mutt want blue noses."

"Okay, okay," Flash said. "We're getting."

Flash and I entered the closet. It smelled like old rags and was just big enough for the two of us.

Brick advanced carefully toward the closet, keeping his eye on us the whole time. "Have fun!" he said. Then he slammed the closet door.

We were plunged into tar-black darkness. We heard a key rattle in the lock.

"Locked in," Flash said. He tried to crash open the door with his shoulder, but after three tries he stopped and rubbed his arm. The door was brick solid. I barked four or five times, but the barks were so loud inside the closet I stopped.

On the other side of the door we heard Brick Glick run out of the room, leaving us trapped in the dark, cramped closet... maybe forever.

Eighteen: Someone says *Shhhhhhhhh*

"What'll we do?" Flash said with a broken voice.

It was so dark that I couldn't see if Flash was crying or not. But when I heard him sniff, I knew he was. Then he started sniffing so hard that it got me whining and snuffling, too.

"Darn dust makes my nose run," Flash said.

Whoops. I turned my snuffling into a couple of throat-clearing hacks.

"Dust getting to you, too, Scratch?"

I found his leg and rubbed my cheek against it. He reached down and scratched behind my left ear.

"Locked inside a stupid closet," he said. "Some detective I am. Am I any closer to stopping this tricks war? No. Oh, boy."

He slumped to the floor, and I laid my chin in his lap. Every once in a while we heard far-off shuffling and tiny explosions and a few hollers and footsteps.

A few long minutes later, I started growling.

"What is it, boy?"

I was up on all fours. The way this house echoed, it was hard to tell where the sound was coming from, but I knew something was coming toward us from somewhere.

Another hand? I wondered. No. Maybe this time it was a foot.

My nose started twitching and snorting. What was that smell? Then I knew. Rainbow detergent.

Then the closet's back wall suddenly disappeared. Dim orange light glowed into the closet. A thin hand shot inside and latched onto Flash's wrist.

"Eee-yah-dah!" Flash screamed. He flailed his arm, stumbled back, and toppled over me. Both of us, kicking and yelping, fell to the floor.

"Shhhhh—shhhhh—shhhhh," said something from the orange glow.

Flash was on his feet again, furiously pounding on the door.

"Help! Oh, please! Heeelllllpppp!" My crazy barking added to the racket.

"Shhhhhhhh," it said again. "Hey, shut up, will you?"

We shut up. That voice was familiar. We turned toward the back of the closet.

From around the foggy light of a small lantern peered the slightly sooty face of Marybeth.

"You!" Flash said.

"Shhhhhhhhh," she said. "Come with me. Hurry. Come on, and beeee quiet!"

"But—" Flash said.

"Will you come on?" Marybeth said firmly.

We stepped through the opening in the bottom of the closet wall and into a narrow, dirty space. Marybeth slid the back of the closet back in place.

"Where are we?" Flash asked.

"A secret passage behind the wall," Marybeth said. "I discovered it when I leaned against a bookcase and it suddenly whirled around. I couldn't believe it. Neat, huh?"

"Why—" Flash said.

"Shhhhhh," Marybeth said. "I'll tell you later. Follow me."

The passageway was dark and damp. Cobwebs hung from corners of the ceiling, and the rotting floorboards were twisted like petrified snakes. In single file, we followed Marybeth's orange lantern down the passageway, then around a couple of corners, until we were in a slightly larger space. Something chittered and scampered off into the darkness.

"A mouse," Marybeth said. "They're all over the place. Come on. We're going to have a great time watching those two jerks fight it out."

"What?" Flash said. "I came here to stop this fight. I don't want to watch it. Don't you care about Pete? You got him into this mess. He's fighting Brick because he's sticking up for you."

Marybeth shook her head. "No, Pete won't get hurt. And Brick won't win. Because I've got this." She held something up into the light of the lantern.

"Brick's magic book!" Flash said. "Hey, you—"

"Yes. Sorry, Flash, but I came over to your house and kind

71

of peeked down in the basement. Then I saw the book sitting on a shelf. So, I thought, why not take it before Brick does? I walked right in and took the book and left. What Brick wouldn't do to get this!"

"Yeah," Flash said. "So why did you want it?"

An evil look came into Marybeth's eyes. "I want to make things even. Without this book, Brick has no more tricks than Pete does. It's an even fight. It's more exciting that way."

What a brat!

"But—" Flash said.

Suddenly, not too far away, Pete started yelling.

"No! Get away! You can't do that!"

Then Brick: *"I've got you now!"*

"Let's go!" Marybeth said.

We raced down the passageway. Thunder stomped around outside like it was looking for a place to sit down and watch what was going to happen next.

The passageway narrowed as it climbed upward behind the walls of the old Doomer house. The lantern light showed us spiders walking upside down on the ceiling; strange beetle-type bugs that glowed green as they zigzagged along the baseboard, then disappeared into thin cracks; and tiny fiery red eyes that peeped at us from the blackness of the floor ahead, then vanished as the light crawled toward them.

I had stopped sniffing a while ago. The inside of my nostrils felt caked with gritty dust. And I sure didn't want to snort up one of those disgusting beetles by mistake. So I was relying on my supersensitive (and very handsome) ears. But, right now, all I was hearing were our own eight feet shuffling along the floor of the echoing passageway.

"Where are we going?" Flash whispered.

"Shhhhhh," Marybeth said.

When we came to a staircase that was only about a foot wide, we all stopped to listen. The sounds of Pete and Brick fighting were definitely closer now.

"Come on. This way," Marybeth said.

Soon we came to a level space in the passageway. Pete and Brick sounded very close. We stopped.

"Here we are," Marybeth said. *"Shhhhhhh."*

Level with Flash's nose were two small round holes in the wall. They were close together and about the size of dimes.

Thin poles of light streamed through, filled with busy dust from the passageway.

"Get back, I'm telling you!" Pete suddenly screamed.

"You wish!" Brick yelled.

"Hey!" Flash whispered. "They're right on the other side of this wall!"

"*Shhhh,*" Marybeth said. "That's right. Take a gander through those two holes."

Flash put his eyes up to the two holes. They were a perfect fit. He gasped and pulled back. "They're right there!" he whispered.

"Neat, isn't it?" Marybeth said. "On this other side of the wall is a painting of some man in uniform. These holes are cut out of his eyes.

"Spy holes!" Flash said.

From the other side of the wall came a horrible whizzing explosion. Pete yelped and Brick laughed. Then we heard Brick holler, *"Whoa-whoa—whooooaaaaaa!"* Then, *KA-THUNK!* Brick had slipped on something and fallen to the floor. "Take *that!*" Pete yelled.

"Hold this," Marybeth said to Flash. She gave him the lantern. "Now watch this. Go on, Flash, put your eyes up there and watch what happens."

Flash pressed his eyes to the holes in the wall. Marybeth cupped her hands against the wall, then spoke into them in the deepest voice she could.

"Leave ... or ... die!" she said. The wall must have acted like some kind of speaker, because the words sounded like a giant fifty feet tall was screaming.

The scuffling from the other room stopped.

"What was that?" Pete said.

"Leave ... or ... die!" she bellowed again. *"You are invading the Land of the Dead! The ... DEAD!"*

Pete started to whimper.

"They're scared," Flash whispered.

Marybeth smiled widely.

"Mortals do not belong here! You are being watched! Leave ... or ... DIE!"

"Look!" Pete screamed.

"Where?" Brick said.

"The—the—the picture!"

73

"Yaaaaaaa!" Brick cried. *"Eyes!"*

I didn't have to be looking through the holes to know what was happening. Running footsteps pounded on the floor in the other room. Oofs and sobs came from both Pete and Brick as they took off for their lives.

Flash leaned down to Marybeth. "They ran like rabbits," he said.

Marybeth spritzed a laugh and laughed harder and harder. She sure was enjoying this. Maybe too much.

"Yeah, that worked really fine," Flash said to her. "But they're still fighting out there."

"So?" Marybeth said.

"So," Flash said. "I want to stop this fight. I don't want to join it or scare them even more."

Then a huge crash echoed through the house. Pete yelled in terror.

"Come on!" Marybeth said. She was having the time of her life, and Pete was fighting for his. And we couldn't do anything.

Nineteen: Stuck

We hurried down the passageway, trying to keep track of where Pete and Brick were going. Every once in a while we'd come to another peephole, and Marybeth would take a look. She saw Brick grab a doorknob that squirted water all over him. He cursed Pete and moved on. We saw Pete turn a corner and walk right into a sudden swarm of feathers. He brushed himself off, cursed Brick, and moved on. The more the guys fought, the madder they became.

Marybeth stopped. She leaned down and picked up a string. At the end of the string were more strings. At the end of each of those strings were rectangular shapes of glass.

"Wind chimes," said Flash.

I knew then that the tinkling music we heard before must have been made by these wind chimes by Marybeth.

"I found them downstairs," she said. Then she giggled.

She held the wind chimes high and blew on them, then thumped them a little with her finger. Tinkle, tinkle, tinkle echoed all over the place.

She laughed when Pete and Brick screamed and ran in the opposite direction.

"Spooky, huh?" she said. "They think I'm a ghost or something."

"I think Pete's heading for the front door!" Flash said. "Maybe your tricks will scare them out of this fight!"

Marybeth didn't look too happy about that. She put the chimes back on the floor.

We took off and soon came to a short staircase, pounded down it, then opened the door at the bottom. We stepped out into a large room with a wide, curved window at the other end. Lightning flashed, and thunder thudded.

"They're gone, I know they are," Marybeth said.

"I hope so," Flash said. "Where are we?"

"We're downstairs on the first floor," Marybeth said.

"Let's see if they really did leave," Flash said.

We walked to the left into a short hallway.

Spak!

Flash jumped back. "What was that?"

Spak! Spak—spak!

"Something smells horrible!" Marybeth said.

Spak! Spak! Spak—spak—spak!

I yelped and wrinkled my nose. The smell was like dead birds.

"We're stepping on something stinky that's exploding!" Flash said.

Spak! Spak!

"Stop!" Marybeth said. "Stand still."

We stopped. Marybeth and Flash were holding their noses. I was holding my breath. Marybeth lowered the lantern and shone its golden glow over the floor.

"Little pellet things," Flash said, still holding his nose and sounding like a duck. "Stink pellets! Hundreds of them. Every time we step on them, they explode and let loose their smell. And they're getting bigger!"

"You bet they are," a voice came from behind us.

We slowly turned around. There was Brick Glick, standing there with his hands on his hips, his sleeves over his hands.

"Brick!" Flash said. "This is your trick!"

"Great, isn't it?" he said. "You fell right into my trap! The more you walk, the bigger the pellets get. And if you happen to step on one of the really big ones... *BOOM!* You'll smell like a skunk for the rest of your life."

"Get us out of here!" Marybeth yelled.

Brick Glick laughed. "There's only one way to get out of there."

"How?" Flash said.

Brick held out his hand. "Give me my magic book."

"No!" Marybeth said. "Never!"

"Give me my book, and I'll show you the way out."

"No!" Marybeth said.

"Marybeth," Flash said to her, "you have to give it to him. We have no choice."

Marybeth growled. "All right!" she said. She yanked the

76

book out of her back pocket. She threw the book to Brick Glick. He caught it neatly.

"Brick," Flash said, "why don't you stop this fight, huh? It's all a big mistake, and you know it."

"Did you hear the names Pete was calling me?" Brick said. "I can't let him get away with that."

Brick was as stubborn as they come. Bullies like him never give up.

Brick turned and began to walk away.

"Hey!" Flash screamed. "You said you'd show us the way out!"

Brick Glick turned back to us. He smiled and said, "I lied." He took off and disappeared into a side room.

"I knew we shouldn't have given him that book!" Marybeth said.

"Give me the lantern," Flash said. "Let me try to get us out of here."

On tip-toes, Marybeth followed Flash as he tried to step in the spaces between the pellets.

Then Marybeth shouted, "Watch the one under your—"

And Flash stepped right on a huge pellet. He ducked and waited for the explosion. Nothing happened. He stepped on a few more.

"Hey," Flash said. "They're fakes! Brick tricked us!"

"*Oooooo!*" Marybeth said.

Me, I was already sitting five yards away and clear of all the pellets. I'd smelled that the rest of the pellets were fakes and walked right past Marybeth and Flash. I'd tried to get their attention, but they were too busy being scared. No one pays any attention to dogs.

"Marybeth, listen," Flash said. "You've done what you wanted. You got Brick and Pete here to fight. But now Pete's in real trouble. Who knows what nasty tricks are in that book. It's time to save your brother."

Marybeth thought about that. "I guess you're right."

Flash led the way this time as we headed into another room.

"It's *you!*" someone suddenly said from our right. And the someone was Pete.

"Peter!" Marybeth said.

Pete looked horrible. He was filthy, and his shirt was ripped in three places.

77

"Pete, are you okay?" Flash asked.

"Yeah, I'm doing okay," Pete said. He kept glancing behind him.

"Not anymore," Flash said. "Brick has his magic book back."

Pete swallowed hard. "He does?"

"Yeah," Flash said. "Come on, let's get out of here."

"I—I can't," Pete said. He looked like he was going to cry. "If I leave, Brick Glick will just get me some other time, some other place. No, I have to finish this tonight. I have to win tonight. Besides, I still have some good tricks left."

"Pete," Flash said, "this whole thing is a big mistake. Marybeth set it all up to get back at you for playing practical jokes on her. There's no reason to fight, can't you see?"

"It doesn't matter," Pete said. "It's too late now."

"We'll go to the cops," Flash said. "They'll protect you. They'll deal with Brick. How about it?"

Pete stood there and thought for a minute. "Okay. I'll go with you."

"Good!" Flash said.

We ran. We took a left and rushed out into the foyer. The front door was straight ahead. Marybeth led the way. Flash and I were right behind her, and Pete was to my right.

We had just run onto the large filthy gray carpet in front of the front door when I smelled it. But I had smelled it too late.

"What gives!" Flash screamed.

"Hey!" Marybeth said.

"Rrr-roop!" I added.

We were stuck. We had stepped onto a carpet smeared with Insta-Glue, and we were stuck solid. We were stuck like someone had nailed our feet to the floor.

Pete had been off to the side, and he hadn't stepped on the carpet.

"Brick did this," Pete said.

"How do we get off this rug?" Marybeth asked.

"Unlace your shoes and jump off," Pete said.

Flash shook his head. "Won't work. The carpet is too big. We couldn't jump that far."

Me, I wasn't even wearing shoes.

"It's no use," Pete said. "You can't help me now. There's no escape. I have to face Brick. And I have to do it alone."

I scratched my ear. Pete didn't sound all that scared to me.

Why the heck would he want to go back and fight? I never could understand humans.

"No, Pete!" Marybeth screamed. "Run! Go to the police!"

Pete shook his head. "I couldn't prove anything, anyway. If Brick wins, maybe then he'll leave you and me alone."

"Don't do it!" Marybeth yelled.

Pete turned and walked slowly back into the darkness, like a convict walking the last mile to the chair.

Twenty: Fuzzy Feet

We couldn't sit down, unless we wanted to stay stuck that way forever. Dogs hate standing still. If my feet aren't moving, I sit. I think it's instinct. And right now my instinct was screaming *sit, sit, sit, sit,* but my brain was yelling back *no, no, no, no!*

"It's all my fault," Marybeth said. "I started this whole mess. I'm sorry, I'm really sorry. I'm so stupid!"

"Yeah, you are," Flash said. Then he scratched his head. "What bothers me is why Pete would go back to fight, especially after I told him that you were to blame, that there was no more reason to fight."

"Yeah," Marybeth said. "That is strange."

"How'd you get here, anyway?"

"I heard Pete talking on the phone with Brick. I heard him say that the showdown was here, at the old Doomer house. When I got here, both of them were running around the house, setting up their tricks. I kind of snuck around, seeing what they were up to and watching for zombies. Then I leaned on that bookcase, and it spun me into the secret passage. I had just discovered those eye holes in the wall when I heard you kicking and screaming in the closet. So, here I am."

"And here we are. Stuck," Flash said.

We tugged and strained but couldn't lift our feet off the carpet. From upstairs, we heard little rat-tat-tats and puffy explosion sounds, then shouts and screams. The battle was still on.

"We have to do something," Flash said. "We can't just stand here."

What else can we do? I thought. *Dance?*

Then I heard a dull flap. Marybeth screamed.

There, at the bottom of the main staircase, was the hand,

crawling right toward us. Somehow it had made it all the way down the hall and down the steps. Neato.

"*Uk!* What *is* it?" Marybeth said. "Make it go away! *Uk! Ooo! Aaarg!*"

"Forget it," Flash said. "It's only a toy. A trick. A fake."

"It's yukky," Marybeth said.

The hand turned right and crawled away into a closet.

"We've gotta get off this carpet," Flash said.

The wind gusted and flicked heavy raindrops through the broken window and all over us.

"Terrific," Marybeth said. "Now we're going to drown."

I knew how we could get off this carpet, but somehow I had to tell Flash. Since he didn't understand dog language, I had to think of some other way. I leaned forward as far as I could go, stretched my neck out, opened my choppers, and bit Flash lightly on the side of his upper thigh.

"Ow!" he yelped. "What'd you do that for?" He rubbed his thigh. "You going mad, boy? You . . . hey! Hey! I've got it!"

"Got what?" Marybeth asked.

Flash reached into his pocket. I knew if I bit him there he'd have to rub the spot, then he'd discover what was in his pocket.

He held it in the air. "My pocketknife! I'll cut us off the carpet!"

"Terrific!" Marybeth cheered.

Flash carefully opened his knife. It was a thin, two-bladed job with a lighthouse on one side and words BARNEGAT LIGHT-HOUSE on the other. With the blade open, the whole knife was only three inches long. It would take him about six months to cut our feet off the carpet.

Flash squatted down and began cutting around his feet. The knife was sharper than I thought, and it took him only about five minutes to cut his left foot free.

"Don't move your foot," Marybeth said, "or you'll be stuck again."

"Right," Flash said. He got to work on his other foot, and finally cut that free, too. Then, with the very tip of the knife, he pulled the edge of the carpet toward him until it was at his feet. Then he simply stepped off onto the bare floor.

"Made it!" he said.

"Now," Marybeth said, "If you roll up the carpet toward me, I can step out of my shoes."

81

"Better not," Flash said. "Too much broken glass around here. Let me cut you off."

Flash cut Marybeth off the carpet, then my four feet. We all looked like we were wearing fuzzy snowshoes.

Then Flash fell silent. Something was bothering him. As usual, he began to think out loud.

"I'm still bugged. Why would Pete go back to fight after he found out the whole thing is a mistake and that Marybeth set it all up? Hmmm. I wonder. Hmmm."

From above, somewhere in the house, came Pete's loud screaming. I looked up, then went back to gnawing on the carpet on my feet. They were beginning to itch.

"Who cares?" Marybeth said. "Let's go up and stop them. Come on!"

Suddenly Flash's eyes popped open. I looked where he was looking. On the floor was a tube of Insta-Glue. I knew it hadn't been there before, so it could only mean one thing: Pete had dropped it! Pete had led us to the sticky carpet on purpose! But why?

Flash jumped in a little circle. "I've got it! I've got it!"

Marybeth was halfway up the stairs.

"Stop!" Flash called after her. "Don't go up there, because—"

But Marybeth was gone.

Twenty-one: Defeat for Pete

Flap. Flap. Flap. Flap. Flap. Flap. Flap.

Flash and I raced after Marybeth on our carpet-feet. We caught up with her on the first landing. Flash kept trying to tell her what the tube of Insta-Glue meant, but he was always cut short.

Suddenly, a huge explosion with loud zooming sounds filled the house. Then Pete screamed, and Brick laughed like crazy. Running footsteps tromped into the distance.

"Oh, no!" Marybeth said.

"Marybeth, listen to me—" Flash said.

She bolted.

We flew down the hallway and up a second set of stairs when we heard a loud *POOF!* and a series of bangs that sounded something like firecrackers.

Pete screamed, "I'm out of tricks! Stop! No more!"

Then Brick, "Not a chance! I'm going to teach you once and for all what it means to mess with Brick Glick!"

"Pete!" Marybeth shrieked.

FlapFlapFlapFlapFlapFlapFlapFlapFlapFlapFlapFlapFlap Flap

We ran. Flash kept stepping on the pieces of carpet sticking out around his sneakers, and he fell twice. My feet felt good. I'd been going bare-pawed all my life, and these carpet sandals weren't half bad.

We burst into the large empty library room.

We all stopped.

There, hanging from the ceiling, was a head. Just a head.

"Ukkkk," Marybeth said.

"Arrrr," Flash said.

Their faces were sheet-white.

Suddenly, the head's dark eyes flew wide. Its drooling, toothless mouth opened. It said in a hollow, deep voice:
"BE ... GONE!"

Marybeth grabbed her hair and screamed just like the young women in horror pictures do. She stumbled back into Flash, who had fallen behind her when he tried to run away. They grappled and crawled, climbing over each other toward the doorway. Me, I was already waiting in the other room.

Soon they joined me. They sat with their backs against the wall, breathing heavily. Both of them were pale and shaking.

"What *was* that thing?" Marybeth said. "It looked like a zombie head."

"It had to be another trick," Flash said. "I know it was."

Sure, I thought. Tell that to Johnny and George Jones. Aroo!

"Whew!" Marybeth said. "A trick. Of course."

Flash said, "Listen, Marybeth, I *have* to tell you something really important. See—"

"Helllp!" came a voice from upstairs. *"No! No! HELLLLLLLLLLLP!"*

"Pete!" Marybeth said. "Come on!"

Marybeth led the way. We bolted through two more rooms, then up another staircase.

"Helllllllp ..."

"He's getting weaker!" Marybeth said. "This way!" She turned right down the hallway.

Then we heard a sound that I felt in my spine. It was a loud *CRRR-AK!* like lightning. But this sound had come from the room at the end of the hall. We raced like crazy to get there.

We burst into the room.

"Pete!" Marybeth screamed. Then her hands flew up to her mouth.

"Holy smoke!" Flash said.

I couldn't believe my eyes. It was worse than I ever thought it would be.

Smeared all over the side wall was some kind of thick black ooze. In the center of it all, slowly sliding to the floor, was Pete. On the other side of the room stood Brick Glick. In his hand was some kind of steel wand. The wand was still pointing at Pete.

"I—I didn't think it would be so p-powerful," Brick said. "I—I only meant to scare him. Honest."

Marybeth rushed up to Pete. "Pete?" She shook him a little. Pete didn't move. Then she shook him harder. "Pete!"

Flash and I ran up beside Marybeth.

Marybeth whirled around to Brick. "He's dead. *Dead!*"

"Marybeth!" Flash said. "Will you listen? I've got to tell you—"

"Pete! Oh, Pete!" Marybeth cried. "Pete, I'm sorry, I'm so sorry. It was all my fault. This whole thing is all my fault."

Marybeth was a wreck. It was time for Flash to act. And he did.

Flash stood up in the center of the room. All eyes went to him. "It's all over," Flash said. "The final trick is on you. It's not so funny now, is it...*Pete!*"

Pete just lay there. I went over and licked his face. Then a burst of laughter came from Pete's lips: *"Pffffffffft!"*

Then Brick sputtered, *"Tzzzzzzzzzzzt!"*

Pete began slapping his hand on the floor. *Fffft!* Great! Great!"

"I knew it!" Flash said.

I was proud of him.

Now Brick was laughing so hard he couldn't even stand up. He leaned back against the wall and allowed himself to slide to the floor, doubled up in explosions of laughter.

Pete rolled over and over, all the time pointing a finger at Marybeth. "Got you! Got you!"

"Huh?" Marybeth said.

"That's what I was trying to tell you," Flash said. "It was all one huge trick—on *you!*"

I barked twice.

"We—we—we—" Pete said. He couldn't even talk he was laughing so hard. He pointed at Marybeth again. "We—we —we knew what you were doing right from the beginning!"

"Ruh-ruh-right!" Brick Glick said. "The joke's on you, Marybeth!"

"Hey!" Pete hollered to Brick. "Did you see her face when she saw me dead?"

"Yeah!" Brick boomed, then spritzed a new wave of red-faced laughter. "That'll teach you, Marybeth, to mess with us!"

"Yeah!" Pete said. "You tried to trick me into fighting Brick. But you can't trick a trickster, little sister!"

"Now hold it!" Marybeth said. "What do you mean, you knew what I was doing?"

"We—we—we," Pete said, still laughing, "we knew all along you were trying to get us to fight! When did you catch on, Flash?"

Flash cleared his throat. "Pretty early," he lied. "But I was absolutely sure when I told you the fight was all Marybeth's fault, but you went back to the fight, anyway. Plus, you dropped the tube of Insta-Glue. Then I knew you got us stuck on the carpet on purpose, to keep us from leaving. You wanted us to stay so you could pull this big trick on Marybeth and teach her a lesson. Simple, really."

"Bingo!" Brick yelled. "Hey, Pete, Marybeth's stupid pranks were really something, huh? The smoke bomb!"

They both laughed like crazy.

"The missing brother lie!" Pete yelled back.

They laughed even hareder.

"The wind chime music a-a-and the deeeeeep voice!" Brick hollered.

They pounded their fists into the floor.

"Aaaaannnnnnd!" Pete screamed at the top of his voice, "the eeeevil magic book!"

That sent them rolling around the floor.

Flash couldn't help it. His lips puckered out and a big burst of ha-ha escaped. *"Braaaaa-haaaaaa-haaa-ha-ha!"*

I started yukking, too. What a gag! Sure, it was a mean gag, but Marybeth deserved it.

"I don't think it's so funny!" Marybeth yelled.

"We do!" Pete said.

"Stop it!" she boomed.

Flash stumbled his laughing way over to Brick. "Hey, Br-Brick. Those tricks of yours were great! You too, Pete. Just great!"

Everybody—except Marybeth—laughed a new wave of laughter.

"Those spiders!" Flash said.

All nodded and laughed.

"And the crawling hand!"

All spritzed.

"And the stink pellets!"

All laughed and said "Yeah-yeah-yeah!"

"And—and—and," Flash said loudly, "and that horrible zombie head hanging from the ceiling!"

Like a record player that was suddenly unplugged, the laughter stopped.

Brick looked at Pete, then up at Flash. "What head?"

We were all out of that place in a second-and-a-half.

Twenty-two: Back to the Basement

The next morning Flash Fry, Private Eye, was in his office in the basement of his house. There was a handsome bulldog curled up on the floor beside the desk, gnawing at the few carpet clumps that still remained on his pads. That's me. My name's Scratch, Fuzzy Nose.

Flash found a new toy. A cassette tape recorder. He had his feet propped up on his desk, his large green hat tipped back on his head, and the tape recorder's microphone an inch from his mouth. He was cocky. He thought the case was a blasting success.

I found my bubble gum that someone had kicked behind a cabinet. I spread out on the floor and chewed and listened.

"It took us only two days to solve this baffling case," Flash said. He shut off the microphone and thought, then turned it back on when he was done. "In short, we did our legwork, gathered the clues, compiled the evidence, went to the scene, and cracked the mystery wide open. My folks were kind of mad that I disappeared last night, but that's the price one has to pay for success in this business."

He shut off the microphone again, cleared his throat, settled in, and flicked the mike back on. I was trying really hard not to laugh.

"Yes," he said, "Marybeth thought she was pretty smart. She really thought she'd get back at Pete. But she didn't count on the famous Flash Fry, Private Eye, figuring it all out. And Brick and Pete didn't count on me figuring out their trick, either. Once Brick and Pete knew that Marybeth was out to get them, they got together to play a joke on her at the Doomer house. Fortunately, I ruined their big joke before Marybeth was hurt too much. She sure did learn a lesson, though.

"A couple of minor points of interest. Brick and Pete later said that they were surprised that I was suddenly in the middle of things, poking around, uncovering their masterful practical joke on Marybeth. At first they wanted me off the case. But then they decided to try to pull the joke on me, too. That's why Pete called me up at night—he wanted to lure me to the ghost house. When I went, they tried all sorts of tricks to scare me, but I didn't fall for any of them. Even though I wasn't scared for one minute in that house, I don't think I'll be going back there again, probably as long as I live. There's a pretty awful zombie head hanging around in there. All in all, I'm proud of myself. And everyone learned a tough lesson about joking around. Ahhh! A successful case feels really good."

I had to run outside before Flash heard me laughing. I scared the birds with my dog-laughter and ate some grass to calm down my giggling stomach. It really didn't bother me that he didn't give me any credit. If it weren't for me, we'd still be stuck to the carpet in the old Doomer house. I rolled around under a bush, sniffed a mole's trail until it disappeared inside a hole in the ground, then went back downstairs into the basement.

"I never could have succeeded at all," Flash was saying, "without the help of my trusty dog, Scratch, Private Nose."

Awwwwwwww.

"If he didn't have to go to the bathroom in the rain, I never would have discovered the kids in the tree. It was because of that astounding bit of detective work that I—"

Oh, geez.

Flash's phone rang. He shoved his green hat to the back of his head and lifted the phone to his ear.

"Flash Fry, Private Eye, at your service . . . Yes . . . Really? . . . That's very interesting . . . Wow! . . . Gee! . . . I'll take the case! I'll be right over!"

He slammed down the phone, dropped his feet to the floor, and stood there adjusting his huge hat.

While he did that, I wandered over and dropped my bubble gum beside my dusty water bowl. I snorted the dust to the edge of the water and took a few laps. I shook myself really good, sucked my teeth, sneezed, then followed Flash Fry out into the bright sunshine.

When Flash takes a case, I have to go with him. He'd never survive without me.